THIS IS MURDER

The nightmare began in a beach hut at White Surf Bay. I was horsing around with a dame called Alice when the guy in charge of the beach huts summoned me to the phone. On return it seemed I had more visitors than I'd ever invited. One of them got rough with Alice while his pal set about softening my skull.

'You mustn't take on the case, Muller.'

'Okay, I mustn't take on the case.'

I did take on the case. But what with the dame's offering turning out to be a poisoned pill and murder being served up as a chaser, I figured it was time I became more selective. But then, like the guy said when he went to meet his mother-in-law, it's easy being wise after the event.

By the same author

YOU KILL ME!

MAKE MINE MAYHEM

THE LADY IS LETHAL

FINDERS, LOSERS

DANGER—DAME AT WORK

THE HASTY HEIRESS

SLAY TIME

GOOD BYE, SHIRLEY

WHY PICK ON ME?

DON'T PUSH YOUR LUCK

SOME DAMES DON'T

THIS IS MURDER

by

PAUL MULLER

ROBERT HALE & COMPANY
63 Old Brompton Road, London, S.W.7

ISBN 0 7091 2088 5

Printed in Great Britain by Northumberland Press Ltd., Gateshead
and bound by Richard Clay (The Chaucer Press) Ltd., Bungay, Suffolk

CHAPTER ONE

I was on a short vacation when the nightmare began.

I was having some fun at White Surf Bay, horsing around in my cabin cruiser by day and horsing around in one of the beach huts at night with— But let me give it to you straight. It was a dame who set the ball rolling. Not the dame who was my hut-mate, because she had already gotten under way with a bang and was anything but a nightmare. But what am I saying? It was this other dame who started it.

She had picked my name out of a phone book or something and put a call through to Harry back home at my apartment, and Harry, believe it or not, had decided to pass the news on to me.

The dame—the one who was nibbling at my left ear like she'd been practising being a vegetarian for a month and was celebrating being back on a meat diet—gave a groan of frustration when the doorbell rang. It was around nine o'clock and we'd spent most of the day playing at pirates along the coast, so here we were, relaxing, kind of, with the lights out and the starshine prying in at the windows, when, like I said, the doorbell rang.

The dame—her name was Alice—groaned and said a nasty word.

'Who the bright hell can it be?' she added conversationally, unfastening her teeth from my earlobe and unhooking ten pointed fingernails from the region of my naked spine.

'You ask real cute questions, doll.'

'Did you clash your dates, by any chance, Paul? Because, if you did, I'm going to tear the hair out of the lousy little tramp that's never mastered the rudiments of self-control, anyway. Go tell her to call on her favourite wrestler if she wants to sweat anything out.'

'Just a minute, Alice baby,' I said. 'You told me you weren't married. Right?'

'So what's with the blue funk?' Alice snarled. 'Of course I'm not married.'

'And you're not divorced, either. Right?'

'You're beginning to bore me, Paul. Get up like a good guy and let me breathe. If I was divorced I'd have to be married first, wouldn't I? Well, I've got more marbles than it takes to qualify for a piece of junk gold that might turn out to be nothing but a chain. Who introduced the subject of marriage, anyhow? And who the hell *is* ringing that doorbell?'

There was one way to get an answer, so I parted company with Alice and pulled on my bathrobe. At which Alice sat up on the bed and giggled at me.

'Keep the bare facts to yourself, whatever you do, Paul. And, sonny boy, like I was thinking if I didn't get around to saying it—don't be long till you're back. I'm a moody sort of gal and it might take me all of a minute to recapture the one we've been sharing.'

You figured that happened only in dreams, didn't you?

I left the bedroom and entered the small hallway. My jacket was hanging there and I transferred the .38 from the pocket to the one in my robe before switching on the light. I'm a guy who's got friends, naturally, but a few of those friends have got enemies. So I was holding on to the gun when I opened the door and saw the night man from the reception office standing there.

He blinked hard at me and rubbed his nose.

'I rang the bell,' he said truculently. 'Maybe six times.'

'Is that all I heard? I had a hunch you were taking lessons with the fire department. What's the beef, Charlie?'

'There's no beef,' he said. 'My name isn't Charlie. It's Hector and there's a gent calling you.'

'Tell him to come back in the morning, Hector. I'm busy right now.'

The mug sniggered and winked understandingly. He was a fat slob in rumpled pants and a T-shirt. He rubbed his nose some more.

'No kidding?' he said. 'This gent's on the phone. He says it won't keep. He wants you to come and talk with him.'

'Didn't you hear what the man said?' Alice snapped from the lounge. 'Go away and ring somebody else's doorbell.'

'Suit yourself,' Hector said carelessly. 'I'll do that.'

'No, you'd better wait, Charlie,' I told him. 'What is the gent's name?'

'He says it's Harry. But don't you give it a thought. You go ahead and call him Charlie. What have you got against calling me Hector?'

'Okay, Hector. Tell Harry to hold on and I'll speak to him shortly.'

'Suit yourself,' Hector said carelessly and drifted away.

I went back to the bedroom and started pulling on pants, shirt and shoes. Alice watched me worriedly, a mean look coming into her eye.

'Where are you going?' she demanded.

'To take a phone call, honey. I won't be long.'

'Do you know where I'll be by the time you get back?' the dame said ominously.

'So long as you dress first of all, baby. This is a conventional-type neighbourhood and somebody might pick you up.'

She let me close the door before she threw something at it. It could have been one of her shoes. Or maybe it was just a leg she had torn off a chair. I hoped she didn't wreck the joint completely, because if she did I might have to call Hector Uncle Charlie.

He was sitting back of his desk, chewing at a cigar butt, when I went into his office. He thumbed to the phone that was off the hook, smirking like he'd stolen an egg from under a chicken.

'Some guys get all the best breaks,' he observed with a leer. I lifted the phone and spoke to Harry Peters.

'Look, fella,' I said, 'I thought I was supposed to be on vacation. Who's paying your tab, anyhow?'

'That's telling him,' Hector applauded.

'You keep out of this, chum. Not you,' I said to Harry. 'Okay, what's the trouble?'

'Sorry to disturb you, Mr Muller. But this party is most insistent that I contact you.'

'Didn't you explain how I'm suffering from nervous exhaustion, physical exhaustion, even?'

'You take too much out of yourself,' Hector said sympathetically.

'I know you're supposed to be on vacation, Mr Muller. I tried to impress this on the caller. But she is very determined.'

'You mean you can't match wits with a dame?' I grated.

'This isn't just any da— lady, Mr Muller. Her name is Marsh. Sandra Marsh.'

'Not Sandra Marsh, the TV star?'

'Gee,' Hector said. 'You do get all the breaks, don't you.'

'The same Miss Marsh, sir.'

'What's her trouble? If she is in trouble why doesn't she get in touch with the cops?'

'A good question,' Hector said. 'But why bother with the

cops when you're around?'

'I'm afraid I can't answer that, Mr Muller. The message she asked me to pass along is this: please ring the Hotel Rialto.' Harry recited a number. 'It will make direct connection with her suite and doesn't have to go through the switchboard. What shall I say if there is another call, sir?'

'Tell her I've had a nervous breakdown and— No, better not, Harry.'

'No indeed,' Hector said wisely. 'The dame wants you, you gotta go. Sandra Marsh? Beat me, daddy, eight to the bar!'

'Listen, bigmouth,' I said to Hector, 'lay off, will you. Just lay off. Let it ride,' I said to Harry. 'I'll handle it myself.'

Harry sighed his relief and hung up. I tapped the phone crossbar and dialled the Hotel Rialto number. I asked Hector for a cigarette and he gave me a blank look.

'You wanta flex your muscles, so go ahead and flex your muscles. What you think this sin-trap is—the Waldorf Astoria?'

I ignored the mug and waited for somebody to answer me. A man's voice came on.

'Miss Marsh's suite. Who is it?'

'It might be the skeleton out of your closet, pal, but it isn't. Say,' I added, 'you wouldn't be taking hormone treatment, Miss Marsh?'

'Is that supposed to be a joke?' the guy raved. 'Do you know what the penalty is for making malicious phone calls?'

'Look, mister, go read a book on adolescence, but before you leave tell Miss Marsh that Paul Muller is on the line.'

'Right below the belt,' Hector said happily. 'I wish I had a cigarette to give you, Paul.'

'Paul Muller? Why didn't you say so?'

'I'm saying it now. Put the lady on the phone.'

'The lady can't come to the phone,' the guy said.

'Oh,' I said. 'That kind of lets me pass, doesn't it?'

'What do you mean, it lets you pass? You're a private detective, aren't you?'

'Yeah, I am.'

'Then cut out the waffle, Muller and get over here right away.'

'Sure,' I said slowly. 'I'll do that. But you'd better find a good place to hide before I get there, chum. You've just ruined the atmosphere for the rest of the evening.'

'Are you sure you really are Paul Muller?' the guy bleated.

'Wait a minute,' I told him. I kept him waiting for five seconds, then I said, 'Yeah, I *am* Paul Muller. It says so here.'

'Where?' he babbled.

'On my driving licence,' I told him. 'And don't forget to duck, chum. I'm pretty mad about now.'

'You're telling me,' he groaned. 'I've got the feeling this is all going to be a horrible mistake. But you'd better come, anyhow.'

'Yeah,' I said. 'I'd better. I'm on my way.'

I went back to the beach-hut to finish dressing. The four walls were still standing and there was no sign of a fire, which wasn't bad at all, I figured. The lights were out when I opened the door and walked in. Alice had gone very quiet or maybe she had really gone away. I shrugged and flipped the hall light on. I was heading for the lounge in order to reach the bedroom when I heard a faint cry. As if Alice was lying down on the bed, hoping to make me feel sorry for her. Then there was a sound like someone was struggling. A shout from Alice.

'Look out, Paul!'

It was all she managed to say. I heard a soft thud, a feeble, drawn-out moan. By that time I had almost reached the bedroom, and grabbed for the gun in my pocket. Not fast enough. There was a quick scuffle of feet, a barked order.

'Don't move. Just stand right where you are or you're history.'

The voice was immediately ahead of me, and I'd no reason to believe there wasn't a gun there also, ready to carry out the promise the guy had made.

I saw a dim shadow in the gloom, a pale face that was pressed into an ugly blob by the stocking pulled over the guy's head and on down as far as his chin. He said nothing for several seconds, just watched intently to see if I would resist the temptation to act the hero.

'You know,' he said admiringly, 'you're smart.'

'Yeah, I am,' I said to the guy. 'Why don't you bring your ideas up to date and join the league? What have you done with Alice?'

'Alice is okay.'

'I can't hear her.' I was playing for time, weighing the chances of taking a flying leap at the character and batting that gun from his paw. The chances didn't strike me as good.

'You don't have to hear her.'

'She might be dead.'

The character laughed. I've learned to judge a lot about a man from the way he laughs. This guy's laugh said he was a heel, the dangerous kind.

'She isn't dead.' He spoke back into the bedroom. 'Let her say something.'

This meant there were two of them. Two at least. Who were they? What did they want? Me? Alice?

What a time to ask goddamn silly questions.

Alice spoke. She screamed. 'Let me go, you big bastard—'
She must have tried to bite the guy holding her, for he swore painfully. There was another thud, not so soft this time.

Alice moaned and then went quiet. The guy facing me closed the door of the bedroom, and everything was very still.

'You're Paul Muller.'

'If you want my autograph you'd better let me put the light on, buster.'

'Back off to the wall.'

'Hey, hold it right there. You're carrying this gag about a half-mile too far. These days you don't just put a man against a wall and shoot him.'

'I'll shoot if you don't do what I say.'

There was the possibility he meant it and I did what he told me. I halted when my shoulders touched the wall. The guy stepped easily towards me. When he moved it let me see how tall he was. He wasn't so tall. Around five-eight or nine. Average build. Johnny Average. There was little else you could say about him in the gloom.

'Turn round,' he snapped briskly. 'Face to the wall.'

'Now take it easy—'

'Do it.'

I turned. Slowly. Reluctantly. He must have shifted quietly and fast for I didn't hear him come the rest of the way. Something struck me a shattering blow on the nape of the neck. Pain. Darkness. The black velvet kind.

It didn't last for long. I came to on the floor and knew there'd be no gun in my pocket now. The guy was crouched down in front of me, holding his own gun aimed at my face. He watched me sit up and shake my head.

'Who is the dame?' he asked gently.

'Just a dame.'

'Pickup, huh?'

'That's right.'

He thought it over for a moment.

'When you drop her tell her this was just a joke. You know,

a laugh. A couple of your pals dreamed it up.'

He really had to be crazy.

'You understand that, Muller?'

'Yeah,' I said thickly. My head wanted to take off from my shoulders. It was packed tight with cotton. 'But look, I must be getting dim, or maybe you're working from the wrong script. The title of mine is Love not War.'

He gave a hard chuckle.

'So who's confused? I don't want to hurt you. I don't want to hurt anybody. I wouldn't hurt a fly.' He sounded so sincere I wanted to give him my handkerchief to dry his tears.

'You're going to plenty of trouble to make a point,' I said. 'What is it?'

'Sandra Marsh,' he said.

'I guess your humour is much too subtle for me, buster. Who's Sandra Marsh? You came to the wrong beach-hut and you don't want to admit it?'

He sighed and poked the gun closer at my face.

'Listen, shamus, drop the bluff. Just drop it. If you haven't been signed up to operate for Sandra Marsh, it's in the cards you will be soon. You're a gumshoe. You work for clients. Sandra Marsh is going to be your client. She thinks. You sign any sort of contract with that dame and you're signing your own death warrant.'

'You know, pal, you've got me fooled. You really have. You and your friend are two great kidders. I'd laugh myself stupid, only you've done something terrible to my head.'

I could sense him growing ugly. I tried to reach a position where I could lunge out at him and take him off balance, maybe. He stood up, beyond my reach. I heard the chilling click of the safety catch.

'That's all,' he said in a constrained voice. 'That's the whole of it, Muller. The rest depends on you.'

It was like being briefed for a dangerous mission into enemy-occupied territory.

I crouched there and looked at his legs. He made a half-turn and I flung myself out in a wild tackle. It was pretty wild, at that, and the guy frustrated it without difficulty. He tapped me on the head for my efforts and I rolled back against the wall and passed out.

When I opened my eyes the lights were on and two people were standing over me. One of them was Hector and the other was Alice. I was kind of surprised to see Alice in such good shape. Still, there was an awful bright glint in her eye.

'Those guys said they were your pals,' she accused. 'Well, if that's the sort of pals you play around with you can count me out of the next game.'

'Me too,' Hector said heavily. 'Rough stuff gets a bad name on the place. What are you doing down there?' he added as an after-thought. 'Say, lady, you sure it was nothing but a gag?'

'Don't ask me,' Alice said bitterly. 'Ask him.'

'He seems to have tripped and hit his head. Did you trip and hit your head, Paul?'

'Sure,' I told Hector. 'It happens at least once every day. Only this time I beat it against the wall for a chaser. Go away and leave me alone.'

'What about me?' Alice demanded frostily. 'You want I should go away and leave you alone?'

'Suit yourself,' I said carelessly, taking a leaf out of Hector's book. 'I didn't plan the gag. And who got the worst of the deal, anyhow?'

'I'll tell you something, Paul,' Hector said seriously. 'I want you to clear the hell outa here in five minutes flat. Get it? Otherwise I'm gonna call the cops.'

I left them and staggered through to the bathroom. I

figured Alice might stay for long enough to say goodbye, at least. She didn't. When I got back to the lounge it was empty. So was the bedroom. All that remained of Alice was the faint odour of the scent she wore.

CHAPTER TWO

It was almost midnight when I reached the Hotel Rialto.

I'd used the time since leaving the beach-hut in getting back to my apartment, prettying up, and finding another gun to replace the .38 the mayhem merchant had stolen from me. I'd used a little time too in making an appraisal of the whole situation. Whichever way I viewed it, the deal was no more attractive than a lonely week-end, and if it hadn't been for my injured pride I might have taken the guy's advice and forgotten I'd ever heard of Sandra Marsh. But here I was, strolling into the hotel lobby that was so roomy it could easily have served as a movie theatre.

The nice boy at the back of the desk had big ears, a white shirt, a carnation in his buttonhole, and a fixed smile on his face that wilted a trifle when I bellied up to disturb him.

'Yes,' he said vaguely, and added after a brief pause, 'sir. Can I help you?'

'Could be you could, sonny,' I said. 'Is Miss Sandra Marsh at home, do you know?'

'So sorry,' the guy gobbled with obvious relish. 'Miss Marsh isn't in to reporters, agents, boyfriends—ex or current—auto-graph hunters, etcetera, etcetera.'

'Say, you're rather good,' I complimented him warmly when he paused. 'What do you do for an encore—charm the perfume off a rosebud?'

He did a double take before fitting the pieces of his dignity together again. He had thin but well-marked eyebrows and the left one was trained to curl into something resembling a question mark that had gotten tired and was lying down for a rest.

'I beg your pardon, sir. I'm merely stating what I was told to state.'

'Okay, buddy. Don't bust a seam. But switch on your hearing aid and get a load of this. I'm expected by Miss Marsh. So stick in a plug or something and tell her you've been delaying Mr Muller for the last two minutes.'

He went into some kind of huddle with himself, then spoke to the middle-aged maiden at the switchboard.

'Miss Marsh's suite, Hilda. Find out if she wishes to see a Mr Muller.'

Hilda gave me a suspicious look before complying. She might have thought I was grinning at her, but all I was doing was wincing on account of the dull pain in my neck and head. She thawed a little as she informed the clerk that Miss Marsh would see me. The clerk gasped his disbelief.

'Seventh floor. Number 712,' he said when he found his voice. 'So sorry, Mr Muller, but orders are orders.'

'Indeed they are,' I said coldly and left him.

I went to the bank of elevators and caught one going up. Everything about this joint looked aggressively plush, the lobby furnishings, the elevator; even the folk going along for the ride had that look of plushness, like they belonged to a luxury class of their own. The hell of it was they made me feel so out of place—as self-conscious as a peasant at a prince's ball.

I disembarked at the seventh floor with the queer sensation of having stowed away on a spacecraft heading straight for heaven and been dumped in midflight when the conductor spotted me. I trod thick carpet pile to 712 and pressed diffidently at the bell button. The door opened a half minute later and a slim, dark man with sleek, well-groomed locks looked along his nose at me. His pale skin was in sharp contrast with his dark hair and dark eyebrows, and there was an air about him that suggested you would have to applaud just once to have him recite a Shakespeare sonnet. Frankly, I didn't like him a bit.

'Yes?' he said in a deep, cultured voice. 'What do you want?'

I had a yen to say I didn't want a thing and to take off on that note, ignoring any further attempts on the part of Sandra Marsh or her representatives to attract my attention. But then I felt a twinge of pain in my skull and gave the guy a quick glimpse of my teeth.

'It isn't what I want, pal, it's what you want. You are Miss Sandra Marsh, I gather?'

'Oh, I see,' he groaned. 'You're Mr Muller.'

'Didn't you know I was on my way up?'

'Yes, I did. But— Oh, look, let's just drop it, shall we? Please come in. But I thought you would have been here hours ago,' he added as he led me through a hall to a large lounge that could have accommodated a teamsters' convention.

'I was held up,' I explained. 'I—' I stopped speaking there to look around me. There was a fat guy fitted into an easy chair like it would take a major operation to pry him loose from it again. There was another fat guy seated opposite him, only this one was on a couch and he was searching in the bottom of a tall glass in a stupefied sort of way, as though he suspected that was actually where the liquor was vanishing. Of anything remotely resembling the Sandra Marsh I had watched a couple of times on the TV screen there was no sign.

I felt uneasy. It just had to be a cooked-up deal. The phone call to Harry at my apartment. The message that Sandra Marsh wanted to see me without delay. The two visitors to the beach-hut and the rough treatment I'd been given. But what did it all add up to? Whipping-boy night in fairyland?

'I'd like to see your licence, Mr Muller.'

'Huh?' I said, curiously watching the first fat guy trying to change his position in the chair. 'My licence? What has my licence got to do with it? And if you're Sandra Marsh, what do they call these chorus girls—Lily and Lulu?'

A pained look contorted the pale features.

'I'm sorry, Mr Muller. I should have introduced myself. My name is Dirk Williams. Perhaps you have heard of me,' he added hopefully.

'I'm sorry,' I said honestly. 'But your face does remind me of something. I wish I could remember what it is.'

His gaze became icy, and when the second fat guy snickered into his empty glass he shot him a barbed glare.

'What do you find so funny, Tripp?' he snarled.

'Who, me? I never said a thing, Mr Williams. Did you hear me say a thing, Sam?' He addressed this to the first fat guy who shrugged his shoulders indifferently.

'We should have a union,' he grumbled and scowled at me.

'Yeah, we should,' the one called Tripp said. 'But how in hell can you form a union with just two people?'

'You could get married,' I said helpfully.

'Now see here, you . . . I've had about enough of you.'

It was Sam saying thus as he levered himself out of the chair. I was willing to bet a buck he'd never make it, but he did. He was about my height and weighed about twice my weight. He lumbered towards me until Dirk Williams inserted himself between us and raised a slim, well-manicured hand that stopped Sam in his tracks. Tripp snickered some more into his glass.

'Go on, Mr Williams,' he said coaxingly. 'Be a good joe and give us all one more drink.'

'No more drinks,' Dirk replied flatly. 'What do you think you're hired for—sitting around on your fat asses and swilling liquor like a couple of over-fed pigs?'

Such words coming from such a splendid sample of genteel manhood evidently surprised Tripp and Sam as much as they surprised me. All three of us regarded Dirk admiringly and a little colour crawled into his pale, delicately-structured cheeks.

Sam shrugged and went back to his chair and I waited to see the chair disintegrate when he lowered his bulk into it. All the chair did was emit a tiny, tortured squeak. After that there was silence. Tripp had given up staring at the bottom of his glass and laid the glass aside. He took a thick cigar from his vest and trapped one end of it between his teeth. Then the two fat guys considered me morosely.

'Now take it easy,' I told them. 'I didn't muscle in here to break up any beautiful relationships. Form a union, if you feel you must. Have another drink if you feel you must. Me,' I went on with an ingenuous smile, 'I'm just going to have a walk in the fresh air.'

I was at the door of the lounge before Dirk Williams found his voice.

'Where are you going, Muller?' he cried in a thin, despairing wail.

'I'm going home,' I said. 'I've had a long, hard day. I've had a long, hard night. Just let's say we all made a terrible mistake and let it go at that.'

'But—but—' Dirk said. 'You can't run out on me, Muller.'

'Want to bet on it, Dirk? Anyhow, who mentioned running? I'm going to walk. It's a lot more dignified.'

'Come back,' he cried as I went on to the hall. 'Miss Marsh wants to hire you.'

'But you said you weren't Miss Marsh. You said you were Dirk Williams. You—'

'You stupid bastard,' he roared. 'You'd better come back here on this instant.

Dirk really was a most surprising character. But then so were Sam and Tripp surprising characters. I went back into the lounge and Dirk told me to take a chair. He seemed at the end of his tether and I was beginning to have a sneaking sympathy for him.

'Okay,' I said when he had calmed down and I had a cigarette going. 'I'll give you the benefit of the doubt. You said that Sandra Marsh wanted me. Only, why isn't she here to speak for herself?'

'She is here,' Dirk said wearily. 'She'll see you in a moment. Just as soon as I've satisfied myself regarding your identity. Now, could I see your licence, please?'

I took out my wallet and let him have a look at the photostat. Evidently satisfied, he inclined his head and crossed the room to open a cabinet. He extracted a bottle of scotch, a pail of ice and a couple of clean glasses.

'This calls for a drink,' he said thirstily. 'What will you have, Mr Muller—Scotch on the rocks?'

'How about a gin and tonic?' I suggested, wondering if he had a hoard of the stuff hidden away in the cabinet.

He smiled sheepishly and said he would have to call room service if Scotch wouldn't suit. He seemed to have a thing about calling room service. I told him not to bother and that Scotch would suit. He fixed two drinks in the glasses and gave me one of them, then he told Tripp to help himself and Sam. Tripp came off the couch like he'd been shot from a catapult, grinning from ear to ear.

With everybody holding a drink we looked at each other. Dirk raised his glass solemnly, making the most of his theatrical training. He was a perfect ham, if ever I'd seen one.

'Let's drink to Miss Marsh's health,' he proposed.

'I'll drink to that,' Tripp crowed. 'But don't forget, Mr Williams, when we're around no harm can come to Miss Marsh.'

At this juncture I began to see a glimmer of light.

'Are you two supposed to be Miss Marsh's bodyguards?'

'What if we are?' Sam demanded belligerently. 'You think it's funny, maybe?'

'I didn't say it was funny.' I looked at Dirk. 'I'm a guy with loads of patience, pal, but you must admit you're leaving me out of the picture.'

'We want to hire you,' Dirk said generously. 'We didn't go into this with our eyes closed, you must understand. Every angle was carefully calculated. However, it was Miss Marsh herself who made the final decision.'

'I'm a private detective,' I reminded him.

'Of course you're a private detective.'

'I was on a vacation.'

'I know, Mr Muller. I know! But once Sandra makes up her mind she must have something, then nothing on earth can possibly dissuade her.'

'I see,' I said slowly. 'Then you tried?'

'Yes, I did. I did my best to impress on her that the arrangements I have made are adequate. But she wouldn't listen.'

'How did she hear about me?'

'Someone recommended you, I believe,' Dirk said dubiously.

It was getting crazier by the minute. But there are two sides to every story, a bright side, maybe, and a dark one. I'd had a glimpse of the dark side and I wasn't exactly hilarious about it. Still, if there were better things to come, I might as well stick around and see what they amounted to.

'Okay,' I said carelessly, 'so let's get started.'

'Fine, Mr Muller. Fine! First of all let me introduce you to these two gentlemen,' Dirk Williams said belatedly. 'That is Sam Walton and that is his partner, Jude Tripp.'

'Hiya, Jude. Hiya, Sam. Now look, Dirk,' I went on briskly, 'you might be able to make a big impact on television standing still and keeping everybody in suspense, but there is such a thing as real life, and I happen to be involved in it even if you figure you're not. So how about a little action on the side?'

Dirk ran one of his slim hands over his head. He was getting that harried look about him again. He appeared to reach some sort of decision.

'Excuse me, Mr Muller. I'll be back in a moment.'

He went off to a door and vanished through it, closing the door firmly behind him. Sam Walton shifted in his chair and fixed me with his grey, close-set eyes.

'What can you do that we can't do, Muller?' he said huffily. 'I mean, we go everywhere with Miss Marsh. We see that nobody harms her, touches her, even. What else can anybody do?' he added reasonably.

'Somebody wants to do her harm? Hey—' I said when the thought occurred to me, '—has somebody done her harm already? Is that what all the—'

'Of course not,' Sam said pityingly. 'Would we be employed to look after Miss Marsh if we had already let something happen to her?'

'But you don't know, do you? You can't be sure? How long is it since you saw Miss Marsh? Has Dirk got her locked up someplace. Say!' The inspirations were hitting me from every angle. 'She hasn't flipped her lid?'

'You're nuts yourself, Muller,' Sam grated. 'She's as sane as I am; saner, even.'

'She isn't ill?'

Jude was about to answer me when Sam made a motion that silenced him.

'Let Dirk give it to him straight,' he advised. 'We don't get paid for shooting off our mouths.'

'You get paid for precious little, it seems to me, Sam.'

The big guy began to look ugly.

'A comic, huh? Well, how would you fancy having five whole fingers shoved down your throat in a bunch?'

I didn't get a chance to reply to that one. The door which Dirk had used for his vanishing trick opened again and Dirk stepped out. He was smiling now, like he had gone in there to make a quick personality swop. He closed the door gently behind him and adopted a dramatic pose.

'It's all fixed up, Mr Muller,' he said smugly. 'You're practically hired.'

'That so?' I murmured, intrigued at the very idea. 'By Miss Marsh, too? What rate does she pay by the hour?'

A faint scowl edged in on his good humour. He raised a forefinger for silence.

'As you no doubt have managed to grasp, Mr Muller, the prospect of having you around is anything but appealing to me. Certainly additional strain is going to be put on my endurance. Please don't make yourself more bothersome than is absolutely essential.' He drew back his lips to show me his teeth. 'We'll play the game with each other, eh?'

'I'll try and remember that, Dirk. But why can't you let Miss Marsh speak for herself? You haven't murdered her and hacked her body into pieces, I hope?'

The guy's face blanched. Before replying he shot a glance at Sam and Jude, wondering, likely, if they'd said anything he didn't want them to say. They both gazed blankly back at him and he cleared his throat.

'I must treat your cheap, tasteless joke with the contempt it deserves, Mr Muller. And now, if we can—'

At that moment the door that Dirk had come through opened and a dame stood there, staring at me. She was small and blonde, with a body that was perfectly proportioned. A real dream baby.

'Mr Paul Muller?' she said at the end of a long silence. 'Will you please come this way?'

'But, Gale,' Dirk Williams objected, 'I haven't got round to explaining everything to Mr Muller.'

'You've had plenty of time to explain,' the blonde retorted coolly. 'Anyhow, Sandra feels capable now of talking to him herself. Come, Mr Muller.'

She smiled when she addressed me again, and it was like a ray of bright sunshine stealing into a room full of shadows. I followed her through the door and found myself in a king-size bedroom. There was a dame seated at a dressing-table and our eyes collided in the ornate looking-glass. The spell lasted five seconds.

'Here he is, Sandra. Apparently Dirk has been somewhat slow about filling in all the details. Mr Muller, meet Miss Sandra Marsh.'

She swivelled her stool round until she was facing me. I'd never seen Sandra Marsh in the flesh, so I had only imagined the sort of treat that was in store for me. Even then my imagination was proved hopelessly inadequate.

I had underestimated—boy, how I had underestimated!— but the surprise was all the more pleasant on account of this. Think of 38, 23, 38, and you might do something real silly like trying to add them together. Distributed over the ensemble that hit my optic nerves just then those figures spelled out the very essence of the kind of poetry I go for.

Her breasts didn't merely jut at you: they constituted an aggressive challenge. Her hips flowed out from her waist like the lower end of an hour-glass. The legs were sensational. When my gaze travelled back to her eyes I saw they were a fascinating mixture of green and hazel.

She had been holding a hairbrush and she laid it aside. She did this slowly too, as though she was under some compulsion to do everything in slow motion. Her voice when she spoke seemed to come from a long way off. It gave me an eerie sensation—as if dead fingers were crawling over my spine.

'How do you do, Mr Muller?'

'Hello, Miss Marsh.'

Our eyes collided again as I spoke. Something was jangling at the back of my brain. Alarm. This dame had just emerged from a drunken stupor, or arrived home from a trip on a dose of drugs.

CHAPTER THREE

Gale made a noise behind me.

'You could take that chair by the wall, Mr Muller,' she said in the same cool voice she had used to trim Dirk Williams' tail feathers.

Chair by the wall. Chair by the wall in this bedroom. A bedroom was where people slept and made love and quietly beat the hell out of each other when they had a surplus of steam to blow off. It certainly wasn't made for talking in. Any bedroom I'd ever been acquainted with, the accoustics were lousy, and rightly so. If you need to talk or make speeches there are still plenty of rooms left in the house for anything so prosaic.

The blonde seemed to understand my reluctance to take the chair by the wall. Sandra Marsh remained perched on her stool by the looking glass. She took a cigarette from a box on the dressing-table and placed it between her lips. All the while she regarded me like I was something of outstanding interest.

'You wonder why we wish to talk here, Mr Muller?' Gale said with that smile which had lured me this far already.

'You're comfortable and cosy?' I suggested. 'Or could it be that you feel outnumbered by the three lads outside?'

The blonde gave a soft laugh, but back of that laugh was a lot of fine steel, I figured. I wondered fleetingly where she fitted into the scheme—if there was a scheme, naturally—

and what her exact relationship was with Sandra of the dark tresses and the strangely remote eyes.

'Did you have a drink, Mr Muller?' Gale said.

I nodded. It was like a game where we were supposed to pretend that Sandra Marsh really didn't exist. Sandra didn't appear to mind. She puffed gently at her cigarette and blew curls of smoke at the ceiling. She watched me go to the chair and sit down. Gale went across to stand by the TV star. At any second now the cameras would roll.

'We've got a problem, Mr Muller,' Gale said.

'I guessed that you had,' I replied. 'But so far nobody has told me what it is.'

'I know. Dirk is so nervous. So highly strung just now. But then we can hardly blame him. You see, Mr Muller, these past six months or so have been a strain on all of us.'

I tried to assimilate that. If she was including the two specimens called Sam and Jude then she was slightly off the mark. I looked squarely at Sandra Marsh. She was peering at the tip of her cigarette as though she wondered how it ever came to be there, between her fingers. With a little shudder of revulsion she mashed it into a tray. Our eyes met once more. She mustered a feeble smile. She was as animated as a rag doll.

'Forgive me if Gale does most of the talking, Mr Muller. I don't feel quite up to it at the moment.'

'Listen, ladies,' I said frankly, 'so far I've done my best to impress on everybody that I'm a private detective. And without wanting to be too prying or personal, hasn't it occurred to you both to call in a doctor?'

'A doctor!' Sandra echoed in a stricken voice. She seemed on the verge of tears. 'There you are, Gale,' she spat accusingly at the blonde. 'I knew I shouldn't have taken those seda-tives...'

'Sedatives?' I said weakly. 'What sedatives?'

'Of course,' Gale snapped in a brittle tone. 'You were under the impression that Sandra was drugged, were you not?'

'Well, nobody told me,' I floundered.

'You're being told now,' Gale said. 'You should be ashamed of yourself, Mr Muller.'

'But I am. I am!'

'As I started to explain to you,' Gale continued, 'we've all been under a great strain; but Sandra, being the actual target of the attack, has felt it most. The problem is, in a nutshell, someone is trying to wreck Sandra's career, to wreck her life. It is the reason you've been called in, Mr Muller. We want you to get to the bottom of the whole dirty deal and expose whoever is behind the campaign.'

Now she told me! From where I was sitting it looked like an old, old story. Small-town girl makes it to the top of the ladder in her chosen profession—and Sandra Marsh really had been a small-town girl—and nobody could deny she had reached the top rung of the ladder. Up there you were wide open for all sorts of stuff to be thrown at you, be it scandal in the shape of a shameful incident you had imagined to be over-looked or forgotten, or spite motivated by jealousy on the part of a fellow member of your profession. It wasn't the type of case I'm keen to tackle and I told them so.

'You mean you are going to turn us down flat?' Gale demanded in a horrified tone. 'But you are a private detective. You take on cases when people don't wish to bring in the police.'

She had brought up a point I was interested to hear them talk about.

'Why don't you wish to bring in the police?' I asked her.

'The reason ought to be obvious to a moron,' Gale said scathingly. 'You bring in the police and you bring in the newspapers. What kind of reaction do you think there would be if Sandra's name was dragged through every cheap newspaper in the country? How long would she last? She wouldn't last at all! Therefore, to call in the police would be playing into the hands of whoever is out to destroy her.'

'That's mighty strong stuff,' I said.

'We're not asking for charity,' Gale reminded me. 'You'll be paid a reasonable fee.'

It was what I was in business for, after all.

'How much?' I said casually.

The blonde's lips curled in delicate contempt. She was disappointed in me; it was plain she was. Well, I did look the Sir Galahad type, I supposed. My reputation had been strong enough medicine to cause them to put out a dragnet that extended to White Surf Bay, and here I was, failing to live up to my image. All I could think of was something plain and ordinary, like money.

Sandra Marsh's features told me nothing.

'We haven't gone into the question of your remuneration yet,' Gale told me. 'Sandra will probably want to discuss it with Dirk Williams.'

'Who is Dirk Williams,' I asked her, 'when he isn't hamming?'

'He's an actor who— But here, Mr Muller, we must get one thing clear before we proceed to the next. You always start at the beginning when you tackle a case, I'm sure? You've already met Dirk.'

'I haven't tackled anything yet, Gale. I'm still waiting to hear the whole facts. After I've heard them I'll seriously consider hiring out my services.'

'Gale,' Sandra Marsh said suddenly, 'would you please get me a drink?'

'But, Sandra darling, drink doesn't mix with the sedatives you're taking.'

'She's right, you know,' I backed up the blonde. 'Drinks and drugs are the perfect combination, only if you want to make a bomb.'

'Nevertheless, I want a drink,' Sandra maintained stubbornly. 'Go and get me one, Gale.'

Gale sighed and crossed the bedroom to reach the door. She halted there to look back at Sandra, something flickering in her gaze that was impossible to pin down. It bothered me.

'The usual?'

'Of course.'

Gale gave me a sharp glance before leaving the room. When the door closed on her, Sandra Marsh seemed to wake up from her stupor.

'You will help me, Mr Muller? You must help me! If you don't, I won't know which way to turn.'

'I'm going to think about it,' I promised. 'When all the relevant facts are at my disposal.' I brought out my cigarettes and offered her one. She shook her head. She looked so beautiful and helpless that some kind of lump got stuck in my throat.

I had a strong yen to go over there and put my arms around her, if only to test whether her vital machinery was still functioning under the burden she was carrying. A dame as beautiful as this shouldn't be labouring under any burden. The eyes were made for laughter, the lips for kissing— But get a grip on your suspenders, Muller. She hasn't invited you here to do a love scene with her. She's in trouble, and all she's asking of you is a lease on your services—professional, that is.

For a moment we sat silent and stared at each other.

'Where does Dirk fit in?' I asked presently.

'He—he's my friend,' she answered hesitantly.

'A good friend?'

'Of course. He's an actor. He got a few small parts in the last series I did.'

'So he's still in the struggling stage?'

'What do you mean?' A little colour stained her cheeks.

'Skip it, Sandra. I may call you Sandra?'

She gave that feeble smile, but it was some reward at least. Despite her condition she was able to react, if only fractionally.

'You feel capable of talking?' I said next.

She looked surprised but nodded. Her colour deepened. 'I'm glad I've got Gale,' she said. 'Gale understands me.'

'But nobody else does?'

'What—what are you driving at, Mr Muller?'

'Call me Paul,' I told her and grinned. 'Look, Sandra,' I went on quickly, 'if you're to be my client it's you I want to talk to. It's you I want to hear talk. Get it?'

'Yes, I do, but—'

'I know,' I needled in. 'Gale. She takes the bruises for you. She wipes your nose for you. But you're a big girl too, honey. You've got your own feet to stand on. You *can* actually stand up on them?' I added.

She essayed a laugh. Well, it wasn't a laugh really, but it did suggest in a vague fashion that vast potential underlying the marvellous superstructure. I figured I might be getting places with her.

'Yes, I can stand up. Don't you believe me?'

'I'm a born sceptic, baby. I've got to see a thing happening before my eyes if I'm going to believe it.'

'Very well!' She humoured me. She stood up. Standing, she was positively statuesque. Once again I felt that old yen rearing its ugly head.

I went across to her and took her into my arms. She did

nothing. She just froze. I brushed her mouth with my own, then looked into her shocked face.

'Come on, baby. Let's have it. React.'

Next thing I knew I was being scattered across the bed. Maybe she had conjured up a mule to kick me. Still, I didn't see any mule when I shook the glaze from my eyes. All I saw was Sandra standing there, caressing the knuckles of her right hand.

'What else would you like me to do, Mr Muller?' she demanded in a furious whisper. 'Rip your hair out by the roots —one hair at a time?'

I was thinking of a suitable wisecrack when the bedroom door opened and Gale came back, carrying a tray with drinks on it. Her mistake lay in trying to take the whole thing in at a glance. Next instant she let loose with a scream and dropped the tray.

'Dirk, come quickly!'

I was getting off the bed when Dirk Williams charged through the door. He was followed by a rumbling that might easily have been made by a herd of wild elephants, but which was actually caused by Sam and Jude. They all crowded into the room and stood staring at me.

It was Dirk who found his voice first.

'What's going on here?' he cried shrilly, throwing countless years of speech training to the winds. 'Muller, what were you doing on that bed?'

'What bed?' I said blankly. 'Oh, you mean that one there?'

'What other bed is there?' he snarled fiercely. 'Sandra, did this jerk insult you? Did he assault you? I told you to take my advice and let me handle it. But what do you do? You have your own sweet way, that's what!'

'You mean she hasn't got a mind of her own?'

'Shut up, Muller,' he grated. 'You've done your worst. You've shown yourself in your true colours. It didn't take you long to get round to it, did it?'

'Let me handle him,' Sam Walton said eagerly. 'You were right, Mr Williams. The minute he arrived I knew he was a phoney. Well, I happen to know how to deal with phoneys.'

'Yeah, you eat them, Sam, don't you. But won't I get a chance to defend myself?'

'Talk,' Dirk gritted. 'But make it fast.'

'Please, Dirk—' Sandra began.

'Stay out of this, Sandra. Leave this to me. Go on, Muller. Explain.

'What is there to explain?' I was standing right by the bed when I had this dizzy turn—'

'A dizzy turn!' Dirk and Gale echoed in unison. Dirk swung to Sandra. 'What about it, Sandra? He's telling lies, isn't he?'

'No,' Sandra said calmly. 'He isn't. He did have a dizzy turn and stumbled over the bed. Why, what did you possibly imagine had happened?'

When she said that, there was complete and utter silence for the space of ten seconds. Dirk's expression was a study in stark incredulity. Gale's eyes were wide and staring and it was hard to say what she was thinking. Sam Walton shuffled his feet and considered his partner lugubriously. Sandra Marsh just stood there, her beautiful features registering nothing, cool and calm and remote.

It was left to the blonde Gale to break the silence. She giggled. Her giggle became a hysterical belly-laugh. Sam Walton became infected with it and joined in. Dirk Williams went over to him and stamped hard on the toes of his right foot. Sam howled.

'What the hell are you picking on me for?'

'Shut up,' Dirk commanded sharply. 'Do you think you're at a circus? Get out of here. You too, Tripp.' He pushed them

out of the bedroom before him. He halted in the doorway
and regarded, first Sandra and then me. His gaze swivelled
back to Sandra. 'Are you going to permit this to continue?'
he asked tautly.

'Yes, Dirk. I am,' she replied evenly.

'Don't worry, Dirk,' Gale said with an attempt at breeziness,
'I'll be right here to see there's no hanky-panky when you
aren't looking.'

'I wish to speak to Mr Muller, Gale,' Sandra said. 'Alone.'

'What!' Gale bleated. 'Oh, Sandra, darling, are you certain
that you know what you're doing?'

'I know what I'm doing,' Sandra told her. 'If you will be
so kind as to clear up that mess and bring us fresh drinks...'

'Of course, darling, of course!'

I helped her pick up the glasses and put them on the
tray. Most of the liquor had already soaked into the thick
carpet, so she didn't have to fetch a cloth to mop it away.
As we stooped together Gale tried to flash some sort of message
at me. I gave her a big wink and she caught her tongue between her teeth.

'After all, I am an investigator, honey,' I murmured close
to her ear.

'A two-bit skunk with bells on,' she whispered back smil-
ingly. 'I just hope you can swim if you get into deep water,
friend. And how come you've got a bruise on your left jaw?'

'I've got lots of mementos, honey-chile. Remind me to
show them all to you sometime.'

'I'll do that,' the blonde hissed, lifting the loaded tray and
heading from the room.

When she had gone I went back to my chair by the wall
and sat down. Sandra had been studying her reflection in the
mirror while Gale and I had been sparring, and now she
turned until we were facing each other.

'What was Gale saying to you, Mr Muller?'

'Do I have to tell you?' I countered.

'If you're going to work for me we must have a solid base to start out from,' she said slowly. 'She didn't believe us, did she?'

'If you want an honest opinion, Sandra, no, she didn't. I'm not sure that Dirk believes us either. But why did you get between me and what I had coming to me?' I added curiously.

'I wasn't so certain you had anything coming to you,' she replied thoughtfully. 'As a matter of fact, you did me some good.'

'Gee willikins!' I said happily. 'But I hardly touched you, even. Just kissed you, kind of. Hardly that.'

'Why did you behave as you did, Paul?'

'Why does the water flow from the mountains? It just naturally flows. But no, it isn't entirely true, Sandra. I read a story one time. It had to do with a handsome prince who found a beautiful princess. But, you know something—the beautiful princess was asleep. She had been sleeping for years, it seemed. Well, this handsome private detective—excuse me! —prince—he leaned over the—'

'You don't have to finish the story, Mr Muller. I read it myself. A long time ago.'

'Then you get the gist. There you were, as cold and remote as an ice-maiden, and I kissed you. And what happened?'

'I came to life?' she said bitterly. 'Did I really, Paul?'

'Well, you were pretty lively when you slugged me, Sandra. It was a start. Still, what gave you the notion I wasn't being fresh?'

She appeared to mull it over for a minute. She lifted a cigarette absently, looked at it and laid it down again. A smile struggled at the curved mouth, gave up the battle, and went

away. Her eyes ran into my own once more, locked there.
My spine tingled.

'I thought at first that you were being fresh. I—I had struck
you before it occurred to me what you were really trying to
achieve. I'm sorry, Paul.'

'Forget it.'

'You will help me?'

'If I can.'

'If it's a question of the amount of money you require—'

'Forget the money too, baby. You interest me. You intrigue
me. The whole set-up intrigues me.'

'But no strings?' she said anxiously.

'Hark to the ice-maiden screaming before I lay a hand on
her! Who needs strings? The only condition I'm making is
that you lay your cards down face up. In other words, the
truth, Sandra baby, and nothing but the truth.'

'Of course. But I wish Gale would hurry up with that
drink...'

Gale might have been reading her thoughts for the way
she popped into the room on the very next instant. She laid
the tray on a table and walked out, not looking at Sandra or
me, not saying one single word.

That Gale was a real keen cookie.

CHAPTER FOUR

An hour slipped past.

I sat there with Sandra Marsh and we drank and smoked and talked. She did most of the talking because, once I succeeded in getting her started, words came out like floodwater bursting a dam.

The trouble had begun six months ago, just around the time Sandra's first big series was being beamed to millions of homes all over the country. Prior to the series she had been doing reasonably well, but if she were to stop a dozen people on the street and ask them if they recognized her, there might be one out of the dozen who would say he thought so, but he wasn't absolutely sure.

The first show changed all that. The series entitled, *Where In The Sun?* was an immediate hit. It hadn't been running for a week before Sandra was swamped with fan-mail, offers from other television companies, offers to make films. One filmmaker said he could put the film industry back in the position it had occupied in the 'thirties and 'forties, if only Sandra Marsh would sign on the dotted line. But Sandra was already signed up, and plenty.

The pilot show was to herald a tentative run of five more to follow. But you can't simply touch a match to a short fuse and then decide you don't want to blow up your mother-in-law at all. The bomb goes bang and *Where In The Sun?* was a bomb.

'You can't imagine the difference it made to my life, Paul,' Sandra said musingly. The drinks she had imbibed hadn't done her any harm. It was a minor miracle, I figured.

'I believe I can,' I told her. 'You made more dough than you ever knew they'd minted. You made more friends than you could house under the one roof—'

'Say,' she said, 'to hear you talk, Paul, anyone would think you'd been with me right from the beginning.' She stopped speaking and gnawed at her underlip for a moment. Her eyes clouded. 'Yes, I understand,' she said heavily. 'You're a private detective. You must have been involved in situations similar to this one. Perhaps you've met other Sandra Marshes.'

'Not a chance, baby,' I said gallantly. 'There couldn't be another girl like you in the whole world.'

'You say the nicest things, Paul. You're a nice guy, really.'

'Thanks, Sandra,' I said sincerely and tried not to blush. 'You're a nice gal.'

It might have developed into a maudlin back-slapping session if I hadn't made an effort to get the train running on the rails.

'You've told me a lot, honey—about your early days, I mean. We've reached the stage where you're famous and wealthy, with a house in the country— You do have a house in the country?'

'A dream house,' she agreed wistfully. 'I'm happiest when I'm there. Hillview. It's ten miles from Burville and the studios.'

'Why did you move into the big smoke?' I said. 'Why Anfield?'

She mashed a cigarette into a tray, took another one from the box, reached for her glass and laid it down again when she discovered it was empty.

'Because of the trouble,' she sighed. 'I decided to contact you.'

'This is where I take an interest in the proceedings, Sandra. I—'

The phone on the bedside table rang just then and the dame excused herself to cross to the table and answer it. I admired her magnificent lines as she did so. Harry would wonder what was keeping me. Harry would be worrying if I didn't get home to my apartment at a reasonable hour. The call might be from Harry.

'Mr Muller?' Sandra Marsh was saying into the mouthpiece. 'Yes, he is here. Do you wish to speak with him?' She frowned and glanced across at me.

'It must be Harry,' I told her. 'Say, what's the matter?'

'I don't know, Paul. The caller merely asked if Mr Paul Muller was here, then he hung up.'

'Oh,' I said. So it hadn't been Harry Peters. Then who had it been? A twinge of pain in the nape of my neck caused a possible answer to suggest itself. I thought briefly of the two characters who had muscled into the beach-hut at White Surf Bay. Alice.

Sandra was standing very still and tense.

'Relax,' I grinned. 'It happens all the time.'

'People ring you up and then refuse to talk with you?'

'Sure,' I said easily. 'Come and sit down. Shall I have Gale fetch a few more drinks?'

She shook her head slowly and resumed her seat.

'That—that's part of what I had to put up with at home, Paul,' she groaned.

'Tell me about it. We were getting along fine.'

'Phone calls,' she said. 'At every hour of the day and night. Somebody would ask for me, and when I went to speak to him he would hang up.'

'He?'

'Yes, a man. Always a man. Then it progressed gradually from there. I would have obscene things said to me. Then threats.'

'Threats?' I urged when she broke off to stare at her clenched hands. 'What sort of threats?'

'They would be to the effect that my career was near an end. That my life was drawing to an end—'

'No kidding? But surely you should have gone to the police. Didn't Dirk ever tell you to call in the police?'

'Yes, he did. But I don't want the police, Paul. I don't want the nasty publicity that would ensue. I tried to shrug it off, to laugh it off. Well, everybody who comes into the limelight has this sort of thing to cope with. Also, as I've told you, I see it as a campaign to break my nerve, to wreck my career.'

I was inclined to agree with her conclusions. But not quite.

'You said it's always a man who makes these calls. Is it always the same man?'

'I—I think so...'

'Then he sounds different at times? It might be another man, or the same one changing his voice?'

'Yes,' she faltered. 'He does sound different at times.'

'Why do you take these calls? Why don't you let Gale or Dirk answer the phone? Do Gale and Dirk both live with you?'

Hot colour crept into her cheeks and she looked uncomfortable for a minute. Then she met my eyes steadily, nodding.

'Yes, they do.'

'You're not married to Dirk?' I said next. I knew she wasn't married to anybody, except she didn't go for anything so conventional as a wedding ring, but I wanted to hear her say it.

'No, I'm not. Not yet.'

'But you and he are going to get married?'

'Yes, we are.' She said this with no trace of embarrassment.

'You love him?'

'Naturally I love him! Such a question, Paul. Would I marry

a man if I didn't love him?'

I wasn't sure what she might do, so I didn't answer that one. Instead I said, 'Tell me about Dirk.'

They had been brought together at the television studios. Dirk was trying all he knew to make the grade, but so far he had fallen far short of the goal he was aiming at. He had appeared in two or three episodes of *Where In The Sun?* Sandra took an instant liking for him and he for her. They began going around together. One thing led to another, and if I could take the dame's word for it, they suddenly realized one day they were in love.

Dirk had an apartment in Burville, quite close to the studios. Success came to Sandra, and her bank balance grew by leaps and bounds. She was ready to marry Dirk if the guy would have her. Dirk said no. I had to hear why.

'He must have been crazy,' I said. 'He isn't crazy?'

'Of course he isn't,' Sandra said with a nervous laugh. 'But he is a man with deeply-rooted principles, Paul. He maintained that if he married me it would appear he was marrying my money. He said we would marry when he too had made a name for himself. He wasn't going to be known as Mr Sandra Marsh.'

'Even though he might never see his name in lights?'

'I had to let him have his way,' Sandra explained. 'I understand him perfectly, and I'm happy to abide by his decision.'

'When did he move in at Hillview?'

'Three months ago. At the time when the threats turned really nasty. I was frightened, even though I had Gale constantly by my side. Dirk has been living at Hillview ever since.'

And enjoying the experience like mad too, I bet. I didn't say so.

'It was Dirk who arranged for the bodyguards?' I said instead.

'Yes,' Sandra told me. 'Jude and Sam worked as security officers at a steel plant close to the studios. He suggested that we hire them. They were hired and came to live with us. They take it in turns doing day and night shift.'

'But they haven't managed to frighten off the lad who's making the phone calls?'

'It's why I wished to ask you to investigate, Paul.'

'Somebody recommended me, I believe. Who recommended me?'

'George Goldman. He's my producer.'

'Then Goldman knows about this too. Why did you tell him?'

'I—I was going off-colour, Paul. Everything was beginning to get on my nerves. I couldn't concentrate on my script. George suspected that something serious was bothering me. He made me tell him what it was. He said I ought to hire a private investigator. Then he said he had heard about you. In fact, he said you were one of the best private investigators in the business.'

'Funny,' I said. 'I've never heard of the guy.'

'George had read some of your books, Paul. He said they were quite good. Perhaps that had something to do with it as well.'

She could be right. I couldn't bank on it. I put George Goldman away in a file.

'Tell me about Gale, Sandra.'

Gale was Gale Bush. Gale had been an actress too, and she had appeared in a few small television parts. Sandra had made her acquaintance when they lived in the same apartment house and headed off hopefully to the same studios every morning together.

'Those were lean days for Gale and me, Paul. But Gale could always be trusted to look on the bright side. She kept me from quitting when I felt so low I was ready to lay down on a railroad tie. "One of these times we'll come up smiling, honey," she always said. I guess she was trying to keep herself boosted, but no matter. Her pep-talks usually worked. We helped each other with our scripts—when we had scripts to learn, that was. Then *Where?* came along and—'

' "Where"?' I interrupted her.

'Yes, Paul. The series. *Where In The Sun?* It came to be so familiar to us we shortened the title to *Where?* Everybody knew what it meant. It helped put Sunrise Studios on its feet, I can tell you. Even George admitted it had the finest shade of gold he ever had handled.'

The dame's eyes sparkled at the recollection. The remote look had left them now and she seemed a lot less worried than she'd been at the outset.

'So *Where?* happened,' I urged when she paused. 'That put you on a pedestal and left Gale exactly where she was when she began. What happened then?'

'An awful lot happened,' Sandra said musingly. 'Parties, invitations, offers; newspaper reporters tripping over themselves to interview me. It was wonderful, Paul!'

'I bet it was.'

She was deviating slightly, but she was well warmed up, so I let her cruise. While she sighed wistfully at some reflection I lit a cigarette and helped myself to the luscious scenery.

After a minute she caught on what I was doing and flattened her hem across her knees. She chuckled briefly.

'You know, talking to you like this has helped me relax, Paul.'

'So Dirk does nothing but get you wound up?'

'Please! We're getting off the subject. Now, what were we talking about?'

'Gale Bush, and how she gave up her career to come home with you and hold your hand.'

Her eyes narrowed fractionally.

'Mind what you're saying, Paul,' she said warningly. 'Gale and I are two very normal girls.'

'Still, she gave up her career.'

'Career!' She made the word come out like a small explosion of scorn. 'What career? Gale never had a career in the first place. Some people make it and some people don't. If it hadn't been for me, Gale would still be running round some producer's crummy couch, not knowing whether she should give in or keep on running. But what am I saying!'

Exactly, honey, I said to myself. What *are* you saying?

'Listen, Paul, you must forgive me. You must overlook that terrible outburst. It was cheap and undignified and totally unfair to Gale. She's a darling, really, a gem. I—I took her away from the rat-race, gave her a home and a job. She acts as my secretary, my dresser, my friend. She helps me with my scripts. Being an actress, she can do that, you see...'

'It sounds a wonderful arrangement to me, Sandra. And she also lifts the glasses that fall on the floor. She lets you weep on her shoulder.'

'What a perfectly horrible remark!' Sandra erupted. 'Do you not believe me? Do—do you think for a moment we're carrying on an unnatural love affair?'

'Of course I don't.'

'You leered when you said that!'

'Cross my heart I didn't. Now look, Sandra baby, if you want this interview to deteriorate into a squalid discussion on morals, then I'm your man. On the other hand, if you want me to come to grips with your problem, you'd better put your dagger away and co-operate. Anyhow, I've finished talking about Gale. Let's skip her, shall we?'

Sandra nodded and looked suitably contrite.

'Forgive me, Paul. Carry on. I—I'll tell you everything I can.'

'Good. Well, so far I've got the picture concerning George Goldman, Dirk Williams, the muscle boys and Gale. Now, to hark back to this guy who's terrorizing you with the aid of the telephone. Are you dead sure you've never recognized his voice?'

'I've no idea who it could be, Paul.'

It wasn't exactly the answer I wanted, but it was just as good, I figured, and probably meant the same thing.

'Okay, Sandra. Another leading question. Is there a man hiding away in the past somewhere—a man you might have known pretty well, a man who might have reason for wishing you harm?'

'I—' she started to say, then firmly: 'No, there isn't.'

'The truth, Sandra, the whole truth. If I don't have it, then you'd better hire yourself another private eye.'

When she looked stubborn I rose from my chair and headed for the door. She spoke harshly after me.

'Wait! Yes—yes, there was a man, Paul. But he would never harm me, or even play a dirty trick on me.'

'Tell me about him, Sandra.'

His name was Al Hoseck. He was some kind of artist who hung out in Burville. He and Sandra had been making pretty hot music until she met up with Dirk and told Hoseck to take a powder. She had posed for Hoseck a couple of times. Nudes? Yes, she finally admitted, the guy had a big thing on nude paintings. She admitted also under pressure that, following her success on television, she had gone to Hoseck to do a deal with him. Result negative. They were Hoseck's paintings. He had paid her a fee for sitting for him and there was absolutely nothing she could do about it. The generous sum she had offered for the paintings had been turned down flat.

'That could be your man, honey.'

'No, Paul, you're wrong. Al might have taken it badly when I broke off our relationship, but he would never do anything so mean as frightening me out of my wits.'

It was her opinion and I let her have it. I slid Hoseck into a file as well. I wondered if the time was ripe to let her in on the incident out at White Surf Bay. But no, it wasn't. If I told her what I'd been put through, she might have a whole flock of canaries.

'Anybody else that might have a grudge against you, Sandra? And don't forget the mutual trust we're striving to get rolling.'

Yes, there was another possibility, she confessed after a lengthy pause. Julia Dortmeyer was her name, but it would be a waste of time treating her as a suspect.

'Let's hear about her all the same,' I suggested.

It seemed that Julia Dortmeyer was an actress too, and a reasonably good one, at that. Julia had a contract at the Sunrise Studios also. When the *Where?* series was being mooted it had been a toss-up between Julia and Sandra for the leading part. Sandra got the plum, of course, and Julia had never forgiven her for it.

'We used to be the best of friends,' Sandra said regretfully. 'Now we practically hate each other. Well, I've no doubt Julia hates the guts I was born with, Paul. Still, I can't see her venting her spite by hiring somebody to stand in for my permanent nightmare. Well, it isn't in her character.'

A lot the dame knew about character. I gave her a warm smile and lit another cigarette.

'I guess you've given me a pretty good picture, honey. Are

you sure you've given me all of it?'

She said nothing for thirty seconds, then she nodded. It didn't take a crystal ball to see she was holding something else back.

'Why were you on those sedatives?'

The question hit her with the force of a bullet. She paled, shrugged wearily, and proceeded to explain.

'The night before last I heard a terrible laughing outside my bedroom window, Paul. This was back home, you understand. The night before that I awoke in a cold sweat and knew there was someone in my room with me. I simply had to go on sedatives.'

'A man?'

She shuddered at the memory and shook her head.

'I don't know. I can't be sure. All I saw was a shadow. It came right up to my bed...'

'What did you do then?'

'I screamed, naturally. Sam Walton was on duty and burst into my bedroom. When he switched on the lights there was nothing.'

'Nothing,' I said drily and puffed at my cigarette.

'Don't you believe me, Paul? Are you going to be like Dirk and Gale, and tell me it was nothing but my imagination?'

'No,' I told her, 'I'm not.'

We chatted for a little while longer. We made arrangements. I would head for Burville in the morning and look around. Sandra and her retinue would be going back to Hillview first thing tomorrow.

Sandra offered me a fee of five thousand dollars. There would be the same again if I managed to solve the case. I said I'd do my best. She said I could claim expenses.

Twenty minutes later I was cruising towards my apartment.

I didn't think anybody was following me.

CHAPTER FIVE

Next day I decided to set out for Burville about noon. It happened that the head knocks I'd taken the previous evening waited until I awoke before really making themselves felt.

Harry Peters, my majordomo, gave me some stuff mixed up in a glass. It reminded me of an old Frederic March movie. Freddy was a friendly, likeable guy called Dr Jekyll before he quaffed the potion he had dreamed up; then he became a really nasty type called Hyde who wanted to rape every dame in sight.

Anyhow, I drank the stuff and waited hopefully for a half minute. Hell, I was still pretty normal and didn't want to rape anybody.

'Look, Harry,' I said in a disappointed voice. 'It's still me. No hairs on my fingers—well, nothing like the growth that old Frederic grew. No baleful gleam in my eyes. Say, I'm just kind of normal. Better get back to the lab, old son.'

'You need a day's rest, Mr Muller. I don't care for what you have told me so far about this case. There is infinitely more to it than is visible on the surface.'

'But I'm a working man, Harry. I took a break and went off for a vacation. But what did you do?'

'Yes, I know, Mr Muller,' he said dolefully. 'I shouldn't have done it. Perhaps it was a mistake. However, you might not have forgiven me had I not passed the message along.'

'You've got a point, chum. So let's forget it, huh? I've got a cheque for five grand. There'll be another of the same if I live up to Sandra Marsh's expectations. If any other clients turn up, you can give them the gentle brush-off.'

I had a big breakfast, read the *Morning Bell*. By that time the gremlins in my skull seemed to have laid off torturing me. Harry was packing a bag for me when the telephone rang. I figured it might be Sandra or some member of her outfit reporting the latest anonymous message. The caller was Alice Ogden, my hut-mate of White Surf Bay. We had latched on to each other at a night spot a few evenings ago, and one thing had led to another.

'Gee, Paul, it's nice to hear you again,' Alice said. 'I've felt ever so mean and regretful over what happened.'

'Me too, beautiful,' I said. 'But we did get to making a little hay while the moon was shining. Have fun?'

'Mmnn!' Alice said reflectively. 'We had a ball, Paul. What I really wanted to know was did those roughs hurt you?'

'Of course they didn't. They were a couple of pals.'

'They were strange pals. But I guess you know what you're doing. Which brings me back to the moment, Paul. When are you going to take me out in your boat again?'

'It's hard to say, doll. I'm kind of tied up at the minute. But I'll be in touch immediately I can. Okay?'

'Okay,' Alice said. 'G'bye for now, Paul.'

I said goodbye and hung up. Then I pushed Alice from my mind.

I left for Burville shortly after twelve and checked in at the Hotel Drury on Second Avenue. I'd promised to get in touch with Sandra Marsh at Hillview immediately I arrived in town, and I did this a half hour later, calling up the Hillview number from a pay-phone in the Drury lobby.

It was Gale Bush who answered my ring. They had checked

out of the Hotel Rialto first thing this morning. Sandra was in bed, and as far as the petite blonde knew, she was still sound asleep. No, there had been no other disturbances so far. Well, they didn't want any, did they? Perhaps, whoever had been playing tunes on Sandra's nerves, had given up the pastime.

'That's wishful thinking, honey,' I told Gale. 'And you know it is.'

'Yes, Paul, I suppose that I do. But Sandra feels a lot happier with you on the job. When are you going to get weaving?'

'It might take a little time,' I said. 'There might be more behind it than meets the eye.'

'There usually is, isn't there?' Gale said with a short laugh. 'She gave you the entire dope last night?'

'She told me things. Maybe not everything. You think she could be crazy, don't you?'

'Well, I—'

'I'd like to talk with you, baby face. Alone. Could it be arranged?'

There was silence for a few seconds, then Gale gave another short laugh. 'Yes, I suppose so. Why not? If you're going to be effective you need to have all the details.'

'And I haven't got them?'

'I don't know ... Look, do you want to come here, Paul, or shall I visit with you?'

'I'd like you to come here if you can make it.'

'All right, Paul. Give me an hour. I usually do a bit of shopping in the mornings on my own account. I'll make the excuse to Sandra that I want to buy a few knick-knacks.'

'I'll be waiting, baby,' I told her and hung up.

I glanced at my strapwatch for a time check, then went round to the parking bay where I'd left the Jag. I cruised around town to make myself familiar with the layout, drove as far as the Sunrise television studios in the western suburbs.

The studios and lots occupied about ten acres. I parked across the way from the front gate and watched it for a while. The whole joint was ringed by a high fence, and there was a uniformed guy at the entrance to see that nobody got inside who didn't have legitimate business inside.

Back in midtown I stopped at a bar and picked up a drink. By the time I reached the Drury again the hour I'd given Gale Bush had practically run out.

I was walking to the lobby when a blue and cream sports car drew in at the curb and the blonde alighted.

'Hi, there, Paul!' she cried. 'Been out for a walk?'

'Yeah,' I answered vaguely, looking from her to the smart sports car and then back again at her. She was wearing a lemon and blue dress that stopped short of her tanned, beautifully rounded knees. The top of the dress was square-cut and fringed with a strip of white that provided the right note of contrast to the deep, golden cleavage which was visible. Her cheeks began to flush slightly under my stare.

'Anything the matter, Paul?' she demanded innocently.

'Wow,' I said.

'Then it isn't serious?' Her blue eyes twinkled at me.

'It can be as serious as you want it to be, Gale,' I said sincerely. 'How do you like my hotel?'

'It's crummy, kind of, isn't it? But then, Sandra should be pleased you aren't going to dig in too deeply for expenses. Where shall we talk?' she added when she accepted the cigarette I was offering her.

'We could go up to my room,' I suggested. 'It's real private, and cute.'

'I'm sure it is. But I'm as thirsty as sin. They must have a lounge bar.'

It was where I took her. At that time of day the bar was empty, with the exception of a character who sat alone on a stool and gazed dismally into an empty glass. We took a corner booth and when a waiter came over Gale asked for gin and tonic. I had a Scotch on the rocks. The drinks were served and Gale helped herself to a healthy swig from her glass.

'Not bad,' she smiled. 'Not bad at all.'

'Was Sandra out of bed when you left home?' I asked her presently. 'She really makes the most of bed, doesn't she?'

'Yes, she was up. The first thing she wanted to know was if you had called. I said you had and told her where you were. When I mentioned I wanted to make a trip into town she asked me to drop past and find out if you were comfortable.'

'Then you don't have a thing on your conscience, baby. Like I was saying a minute ago, does she spend much of her time in bed?'

'No, not really. Only when she feels she needs to get away from everything.'

'She take many sedatives?'

'Only when—'

'Yeah, I know,' I interrupted her. 'When she wants to get away from it all. Her nerves are bad, I gathered.'

'Worse than bad,' Gale admitted sadly. 'I'll tell you what I think, Paul, if she doesn't soon get a grip of herself she's going to finish up in a rest home.'

'So Dirk isn't such a great consolation?'

'Oh, don't blame Dirk for anything. He's done his best for her. He's doing his best for her. If—if only she'd stop imagining that things are worse than they are.'

I had a swallow of Scotch and lit another cigarette.

'The phone calls. Is she imagining they're happening?'

'Good heavens, no! They're real enough. I've taken them myself. Dirk has taken them.'

'They're made by a man?'

'Always by a man.'

'The same man all the time?'

She thought about this for a moment, her thin brows forming twin arches on her smooth, tanned forehead.

'Sometimes the voice seems different,' she said firmly. 'Didn't Sandra tell you so herself?'

'Yeah, she did.'

The lone customer at the bar was muttering something into his glass now. The drink server was standing back a little and eyeing him warily. The air-conditioning hummed. The traffic on the street had slackened off. The atmosphere throbbed with heat.

'What exactly does this voice say?'

The blonde looked at me blankly for several seconds, then appeared to drag her thoughts back from someplace.

'It's hard to remember the precise words,' she said slowly.

'Try,' I urged. 'They aren't always the same words?'

'The phrasing varies,' Gale explained, 'but the gist is usually the same. "Sandra, why don't you quit trying and find yourself a nice hole to crawl into?"'

'Sandra never told me that.'

'No? Then she didn't hear what I heard. But yes, she did. She always makes me tell her what the man has said.'

'He has threatened her life?'

Gale nodded. She frowned. She finished the contents of her glass and I signalled the waiter to repeat our order.

'This is beginning to be a bit of a drag, Paul.'

'What is?' I asked curiously.

'Talking about Sandra. Well, if you go on doing it for long enough, you get to believe after a while that the whole goddamn world revolves around her.'

I had an idea I knew what she meant. Once upon a time Gale had been equipped with a mind of her own and a personality of her own. Nowadays that personality was being overridden by the extent of the trials and tribulations of the girl she worked for. Sandra's troubles tended to outweigh those of anyone else about her. Thus she was more important, more demanding than would be the case if everything was running smoothly for her.

All the same, the blonde had a way out if she wanted to make use of it.

'You don't have to live with her, do you?' I said. 'You didn't draw up any sort of contract and sign it with your own blood?'

'Of course I didn't. What are you trying to say—that the two of us can't live without each other? Yeah, you would think along those lines, wouldn't you, Paul? It isn't that you want to have dirty thoughts in your head, it's just that they naturally happen there and there isn't much you can do about it. Look,' she went on softly, 'Sandra and I are pals from way back. She got a lucky break and I didn't. Maybe it wouldn't have mattered how many lucky breaks came my way. You're either cut out to be a big star or you're not. It's simple.'

'Real simple,' I agreed.

The waiter came with our drinks and Gale made inroads on her second gin and tonic. She took another cigarette I offered her and sighed.

'Why the hell should I worry? I've got a roof over my head that I don't have to pay rent for. I get enough to eat. Sandra made me a present of that car out there. She pays me a generous salary. So what's so sensational about being a TV star?'

'What indeed,' I agreed. 'It seems to me you're getting all the benefits without having to strain yourself further than the limit.'

Gale thought about that and fixed me with her blue eyes.

There was the faintest hint of suspicion gathering in them now.

'Just what are you driving at?' she said. 'You asked me to come and talk with you. Do you want to talk about Sandra, or is the subject of the discussion to be me?'

'I'm being hired by Sandra, baby. You said yourself the world revolves round her. As far as I'm concerned that's the way it has to be until I've solved her case.'

She gave a hard laugh at that, steadied herself, met my slightly hurt stare.

'You don't think I solve cases, maybe?'

'Don't get me wrong, Paul. You strike me like the kind of guy that might solve plenty if you didn't keep your hands tied behind your back all the time.'

I looked at her for a whole minute. Either we were getting our lines crossed or those knocks on the head I'd taken at White Surf Bay had really made me stupid.

'You know,' I said when a lot more time had gone by, 'I've never noticed how my hands are tied behind my back. But you could be right. So what are we waiting for?'

Like I keep on saying, you never know with dames.

We left the bar and took the elevator to the third floor. I had 307, which Gale figured was a lucky number. She took the key from me, opened the door, then prowled over the joint as though there might be somebody hiding someplace.

'What's the matter?' I said. 'Are you nervous?'

'Not really.'

She came back to stand in front of me. The crown of her head didn't reach any higher than my chest. Mischief shone in the blue eyes. The blonde hair glinted like spun gold.

'Gosh, you're big, Muller,' she marvelled.

'Yeah, I am. A healthy appetite, clean living, and eight

hours' sleep every night,' I said proudly.

'Gosh!' she said in wonderment. 'You'd think that would be an awful bore. And look at me. Where did I ever go wrong, do you figure?'

'Sorry, honey. I wasn't around when it happened. But you don't have to worry too much. You made out fine.'

She had, too. All over.

'So you don't mind tiny girls, Paul?'

'Hell,' I said and brought her into my arms, 'I wouldn't call you tiny. And who cares so long as you're all this potent.'

She wriggled free and touched her mouth where I'd kissed her.

'Golly Moses!' she exclaimed. 'Wouldn't Sandra have a fit if she knew.'

'You mean you have to tell her?' I snarled impatiently. If she knew what? That you're tiny? That you're potent?'

'Of course not. If she knew we were together like this—you and I.'

'But I haven't even touched you yet,' I practically yelped. 'Do you want I should call Sandra up to come and hold your hand? Look, baby face,' I went on seriously, 'perhaps it has just occurred to me why you've never grown up to be six feet tall. I mean, didn't you ever have the real lowdown on the birds and the bees. They don't get their kicks from just kissing, for pete's sake.'

'No?' she said innocently. 'But I always was a slow learner, and maybe I've come to the right man to take lessons. Can I make use of your bedroom for a minute, Paul? But you must promise not to peek.'

'Go ahead,' I said wearily and watched her pass through the door.

The door closed. I lit a cigarette. I wondered where a good movie might be showing this time of day.

The bedroom door opened fractionally a few moments later. I mashed out my cigarette and sighed. What did she expect me to do now—play some corny game like I spy?

'Okay, Paul,' Gale sang out. 'I'm ready for the first lesson, teacher.'

I expected a little-girl gag for sure. I was ready for anything but the sight that confronted me when I pushed the door wide open and walked into the room.

Gale was standing there, naked, holding her miniature Venus de Milo body in an exaggerated girlie-mag pose.

'How am I doing for a beginner, Paul?'

She was sheer, unadulterated poetry, right down to the last intriguing stanza. My eyes did a couple of round trips before I remembered I had to go on breathing to stay alive.

'Baby,' I said in an awed whisper as I pulled off my jacket and flung it to the floor, 'the next person calls you tiny I want you to send him to me so I can tell him what an awful liar he is.'

CHAPTER SIX

It could have been all of an hour later when we came up for air. In some situations a guy can be forgiven for overlooking the time; right then I didn't care if the year was 2001. At least the simple pleasures of life hadn't changed much.

'You know, Alice baby,' I murmured happily, 'you're a swell pupil for a raw beginner.'

'Alice?' Gale said tautly and sat up a little. 'Where did you get this Alice stuff from?'

'Did I say Alice?' I shrugged carelessly. 'It must be on account of how you know your way around Wonderland so well.'

It mollified Gale if it didn't actually convince her.

We dressed, had some drinks sent up. And then I remembered I was supposed to be working on a case. I remembered why I had really wanted Gale to visit at the Drury and talk with me.

I didn't rush the blonde. I'd learned enough about her this far to understand she didn't like to be rushed. I merely drew her out gently.

'Al Hoseck? Sure, I know Al Hoseck. Why, he has his place not too far from here, Paul. Paris Avenue.'

'He paints?'

'Sure does,' Gale giggled. 'He painted Sandra. She wanted to buy those revealing studies he made of her, but he wouldn't sell them. Well, money isn't everything, is it? Some guys are sentimental. If Al couldn't have Sandra, then I guess he wanted to keep those pictures.'

'They were pretty sweet on each other?'

'That's right, Paul. They were. Give me another drink.'

'You don't want to get drunk, baby. What would Sandra have to say if you turned up drunk and had to admit you were playing around with me?'

'The hell with Sandra,' Gale said recklessly. She caught the look in my eye and giggled some more. 'I don't mean it really, Paul. She's got her problems already without any help from us.'

That was for sure. I gave the dame another drink. I had another drink myself, not too much; just enough to encourage the warm glow I had in the pit of my stomach to stay there.

'Is Hoseck the sort of lad would let a grudge fester?' I asked Gale.

'You mean, would he be capable of scaring the pants off Sandra? Yes, he might at that. And you could hardly blame him. There they were—Al and Sandra—like two perfect love-birds. Before she met up with Dirk and gave old Al the frozen mitt.'

'What kind of guy is Dirk?'

'A guy is a guy is a guy. I'll have another little drink, Paul. Just a little one. He's okay if you go for his sort.'

She poured the drink for herself, burped delicately and gave me a wry smile.

'You never take your mind off your work for long, do you?'

'It can be a drag,' I admitted. 'How about Julia Dortmeyer?'

'Julia Dortmeyer? Say, you been rolling in the hay with her as well? You do get around, don't you. What size of class do you teach?'

'Listen, honey,' I said and plucked the glass from her

fingers, 'why don't you try doing something with that one-track mind of yours? I never met Julia in the whole of my life. But she is an actress too, I hear. Sandra just pipped her at the post for the leading role in *Where?* Would Julia be tempted to light any kind of fire under Sandra?'

Gale gave a shrill laugh and sprawled herself out on an easy chair. There was something deliciously abandoned about her just then.

'Why not?' she cried. 'But why stop with Al and Julia? Sandra might have told you a sackful, Paul, but she didn't tell you all. Let me put you straight before you start confusing yourself. You might think that Sandra's friends outweigh the enemies she's made. Well, don't believe a word of it. Since Sandra made a name for herself she doesn't care how she behaves. She'd cut her own mother dead in the street if she was in a mean enough mood. She used to have a big smile for everybody. She used to be kind and considerate. Not any more. I tell you, Paul, if that's what success means when it finally comes home to roost, then I don't want any of it, thanks all the same.'

In a way I was disappointed with what I'd heard. If Gale was telling the truth—and there didn't seem any reason why she shouldn't be telling the truth—then the field of suspects was wide open, and I might be busy for the next ten years.

At that moment the phone rang and I went to answer it. Gale sat up and tried to look virginal and sober.

'It's got to be Sandra, Paul. Once you come inside her orbit and she has you on the payroll, then you can expect to be called on at any hour of the day or night.'

It was an outside call and it turned out Gale was right. A few seconds later Sandra was speaking urgently into my ear. 'I've just had another one, Paul,' she said in a stricken voice. 'Not five minutes ago...'

'A threatening call?' I asked carefully.

'Yes, yes!' she babbled excitedly.

'Cool it down, honey. What do you want me to do besides doing what I'm engaged at?'

'That's just it,' Sandra snapped curtly. 'What are you engaged at? When are you going to find out who's causing me all of this misery?'

'I've only got started. It could take time.'

She groaned and grated something that was too indistinct to understand. It sounded as if she might be chewing up the phone.

'Can you come to see me at once, Mr Muller?'

Why not, I thought. It would give me an opportunity to have a look at the television star's homestead. And, as Sandra was paying the tab anyhow, I had nothing to lose. Well, not much.

'Sure,' I said. 'I'm on my way.' I was on the point of hanging up when Sandra said something else.

'Have you seen Gale? She said she would call with you.'

'No,' I said. 'She mustn't have got around to calling on me.'

'Look, Paul, is there any strong reason why you must stay in that hotel? I would prefer to have you out here at Hillview.'

'It's ten miles from town, Sandra. You said so yourself. And what about Dirk and his pet bloodhounds? Won't they figure you've lost faith in them?'

'Listen, Mr Muller,' she said sharply, 'is Dirk hiring you, or am I hiring you?'

'You are, of course, Sandra,' I said meekly.

'Then check out of that hotel and come to Hillview. There are plenty of rooms and you won't feel cramped.'

'I'll take your word for it, honey,' I said and hung up.

By this time Gale was standing at my elbow. She laid a slim hand on my forearm, peering into my face with a peculiar expression on her own features.

'You've been invited to live at Hillview, Paul?'

'Ain't life marvellous?' I grinned. 'Say, you don't care for the idea?'

'I don't know,' she said. 'It could complicate matters.'

I wasn't sure what she meant and I didn't ask her to explain. I told her Sandra had been asking if she'd called and that I'd said no, she hadn't.

'You did the right thing, Paul. Look, I'll wait until you're ready to move and then show you the way to Hillview.'

I packed my bag and rang down to the desk clerk to say I was checking out. Gale left me then, saying she would wait for me on the street. When I got down to the street she was sitting at the wheel of her sports job, looking calm, sober and relaxed. She waved me over.

'Did Sandra have any special reason for asking you to come live with us, Paul?'

'Yeah, she did. It seems she had another of those phone calls.'

'Poor Sandra! That explains it. Get your car and follow me, Paul. If we're seen arriving together we'll say you overtook me on the road.'

I said okay and went to pick up the Jag. A few minutes later we were heading for the outskirts of Burville.

We left town by the north end and used a highway for about four miles before leaving it to drive along a narrow road that slashed deeply into the hill country. I figured I was a pretty fast driver, with a reasonable amount of skill, but the blue and cream sports car kept edging far in front of me until I thought the hell with competition and ambled along at my leisure.

I found the blonde waiting for me at the entrance to a wide, tree-flanked driveway. The wind had tossed her hair and whipped a lot of colour into her cheeks, and the blue eyes had a trace of mischievous mockery in them.

'Gee, I thought you'd gone back to town again, Paul. Does that heap just have hairs on its chest and no muscles under-neath?'

'Sure,' I cracked with an evil smile, 'just like you, baby. But who wants muscles when—'

'Drop it right there, mister,' she said warningly. 'From now on we're going to be strangers, practically. There's enough fur and stuff flying around here without us adding to the confusion.'

'You mean we're not going to continue?'

'Exactly,' she cut in again. 'If I happen to want some music occasionally, you must let me call the time and the tune.'

She ordered me to go on ahead of her and she would hang around the entrance for a while. I shrugged and began to leave her.

'You can't go wrong, Paul. Follow the driveway till you come to the house. There's only one house, so you can't miss it.'

It was a house that nobody could miss. It sprawled over enough ground to take half a block of buildings back in town. The architecture was a curious mixture of Moorish and Old Colonial and it hit the eye like a backcloth to a bad dream. There were wide, lush lawns fringed with shrubbery and ornamental trees, and if a guy hadn't known better he might easily have taken the layout for some kind of weirdo Hotel de Luxe.

There were three other cars lounging on the forecourt where I left the Jag. The sun shone down on them and was reflected straight off them as though their own glory was self-sufficient. The front door of the house was closed and no doubt bolted and barred. I stood for a moment and brought a cigarette to my mouth, then I hiked on to the corner of the monstrosity and round to the rear.

Here were tennis courts, more lawns, and a swimpool big enough to shoot the action scenes in *The Cruel Sea*. Here too were Sam and Jude, clad in swimshorts and having a workout with weight-lifting gear. A little way off Dirk Williams reclined gracefully on a deckchair, a cigarette in the fingers of one hand, a tall, cool-looking glass in the other.

'Put a little steam into it,' Dirk was saying languidly. He was addressing Sam who was manfully striving to raise something in the region of fifty pounds over his head with both hands. 'Yes, that isn't bad, Sam. Not bad at all. Now let Jude have a try.'

'Cheese, Mr Williams, do I really have to?' Jude complained. 'What do I want to build muscles for when I've got plenty already?'

'Why indeed?' I broke in cheerfully. 'Especially when most of them are so well hidden inside of your head.'

'Aw no!' Jude groaned at sight of me. 'The private eye again. Did you never learn to read, Muller?' he went on sneeringly. 'There's a sign round front that reads, "No dogs except on leashes."'

'Never mind, Jude,' Dirk said briskly, lifting himself out of his deckchair and giving me a long, hard stare. 'What do you want here, Mr Muller? Have you succeeded in solving the case already?'

'You mean we've been getting ourselves into good shape for nothing?' Jude griped.

'Sandra invited me,' I said to Williams. 'And speaking of shapes,' I said to Jude, 'did you ever have a peek at your naked torso in a looking-glass?'

'You figure you're smart?' Sam Walton grunted and began

rumbling towards me. 'Well, let's just see how smart you really are, Muller.'

'No, Sam,' Dirk Williams objected. 'We can't have Mr Muller getting hurt.'

By the tone of the guy's voice he'd have given a lot to see me down on my knees, crawling. There was a message in the tone too that meant Sam could go ahead and hurt me if he didn't leave me with visible injuries afterwards.

The punk came to a halt before me and flexed his huge biceps. He had a chest measuring some sixty inches, but there was too much flab around his midriff to make him anything more effective than a walking barrel.

'Sam!' Dirk yelped in a high-pitched squeak. 'Don't you dare put your hands on him. Mr Muller, don't rouse him, whatever you do. I won't be responsible for the consequences.'

'But Sam wouldn't hit an old buddy like me. You wouldn't really, would you, Sam?'

'I don't like jerks,' Sam said conversationally. 'The ones with the loose mouths I hate most. And you know something, Muller, you've got one of the slackest mouths I ever did see.'

'No kidding? But be your age, pal. Get the message. I'm not your playmate. If you want somebody to slap you on the back you've gone and picked on the wrong guy.'

The mug's mean eyes had a baffled stare for a moment. He didn't know whether I was frightened or bluffing.

'All right, Muller,' he said generously. 'Just say you're sorry and we'll let the whole thing ride.'

'Sorry? Who said I was sorry? Whose turn is it to apologise anyway? Really, Sam, you ought to brush your marbles together.'

The mean eyes flared wildly and then something went pop in behind them. I watched it all happening like I was watching a close-up in a movie theatre. The guy might as well have sent me a letter saying his best punch was on the way.

It missed me by six inches and carried on across my left shoulder. Then, while Sam was wondering which country it would come down in, I drove a crisp short jab into his soft, fat stomach. His eyes went glassy with the shock and the pain. Robbed of control, his heavy body did a ridiculous jack-knife which meant he was presenting his square chin to my mercy. I hung a wicked tap on the target and Sam slammed down in a bundle at my feet.

'What went wrong?' he mumbled in a bemused fashion. 'Somebody tell me what went wrong.'

'It isn't incurable,' I told the guy. 'But take my advice and find yourself a new trainer.'

'I will,' he babbled like a moron. 'I will, I will!'

I was leaving Sam when Jude and Dirk Williams began closing in on me from two sides. Jude didn't have a lot of enthusiasm for what he figured Dirk was about to order him to do. At the last moment it seemed to occur to Dirk he had wandered into a role that nobody had cast him for. He came up short and raised a hand to stay Jude.

'No,' he said thickly. 'It might be too dangerous. These private detectives have been known to carry all manner of weapons.'

'Sure,' I sneered. 'Like a couple of arms with a single fist on the end of each. What's the matter, Dirk—didn't you have cream with your cornflakes this morning?'

The guy's tongue darted over his thin-lipped mouth. He broke into a half-hearted snigger.

'We didn't mean anything, Mr Muller. It was all in fun. The boys like to have a work-out every day. I guess Sam's sense of loyalty must have got the better of him.'

At this Sam heaved himself to his haunches and glared at the bad actor.

'Oh, yeah!' he snarled. 'Well, I've got a good mind to quit. As for you,' he bleated at Jude, 'why didn't you come to my aid?'

'Don't blame Jude,' I told Sam. 'He just figured you'd need lots of room to swing, and boy, did you swing!'

Whatever might have ensued was precluded by the arrival of Sandra Marsh on the scene. She was wearing a dark silk sheath that fitted her like a double skin, and she had come across the patio to stand and stare at us.

'Mr Muller, you've arrived! You should have come to the front door.' Then she noticed Sam and her eyebrows rose. 'What on earth happened to you, Sam?'

'He was messing about with those weights,' I explained. 'The trouble is he doesn't know his own strength.'

The green, hazel-flecked eyes centred on Dirk Williams.

'I told you not to take too much out of the boys, Dirk. All that exercise in the hot sunshine can't be good for them.'

Dirk just glared like he'd been struck dumb. Sandra made a motion with her hand. Jude had a quiet snicker to himself.

'Please come inside, Mr Muller. Did you bring any baggage?'

'Baggage!' Dirk spluttered then. 'Sandra, you—you don't mean that Mr Muller is coming here to stay?'

'It's exactly what I do mean, Dirk. Do you have any objections to offer?'

'Yes, I have,' the actor said heatedly. 'I think you're making a dreadful mistake.'

'Do you now? Well, Mr Muller is here and here he is going to remain until this whole trouble is cleared up.'

She took me over the patio, into a long, narrow hall that was cool and somehow insulated from the world outside. We finished up in a large living-room where she asked me to sit down and wondered if I'd like a drink. I said I would and she rang a bell that roused a middle-aged houseboy. His name was Hackett, Sandra explained when he'd gone off to fix the Scotch I ordered. Besides Hackett there was a maid called Petra, and a cook called Collins.

'You've got yourself quite a household, honey, and I just bet you never get a chance to feel lonesome.'

She shuddered as though I'd made a distasteful gag. She made no comment. We sat on two overstuffed chairs and looked at each other until the drinks arrived.

'Thank you, Hackett,' she told the houseboy. 'Now, would you please take Mr Muller's baggage from his car and bring it up to the guest room in the east wing?'

'Of course, Miss Marsh,' the guy said dutifully and left the room with no more sound than a fly would make walking on the ceiling.

We sipped our drinks and I lit a cigarette. I heard a car draw up outside and guessed the newcomer was Gale Bush. Sandra Marsh spoke swiftly then, in a voice that was little above a hoarse whisper.

'As I've already told you, Paul, I had another phone call, and I don't mind telling you I'm scared half to death.'

'You don't have to tell me, baby. I can see for myself. What did the guy have to say this time?'

'He—he—' She broke off to take a hefty swig from her glass, then she fixed me with a stare that set my nerves to tingling. 'He said I hadn't much longer to live. He said the curtain was all set to fall on the final act, and I'd better get ready to take my last bow... Paul, you must help me. You must do something before it's too late to save me!'

CHAPTER SEVEN

It seemed the best plan was to take the threats seriously and behave as though Sandra Marsh might soon be viewed by her tormentor over the sights of the gun he would use to kill her, It seemed too that it was reasonable to assume the potential killer's weapon would be a gun. The grounds of Hillview were lying wide open for a whole squad of killers to come lurking in the trees and shrubbery and stuff.

I talked this over with Dirk Williams, not because I wanted to, or figured he would be in any way effective if it came to the pinch, but because I felt it necessary to form some sort of cohesive effort, where the right hand would know what the left hand was doing, so that Sandra would have the full benefit.

The guy's reaction was typically smug and stupid.

'Who do you think you are, Mr Muller?' he said sneeringly. 'General Grant? I know what I'm doing, and if you knew what you were doing, everything would go along fine.'

'But this isn't a TV rehearsal,' I grated at the punk. 'This is real life, and somebody is out to kill Sandra. Don't you want her to have all the protection that's going?'

He gave me a sharp glance at that, started to say something nasty, but changed his mind at the last moment. A glimmering of suspicion entered his dark eyes.

'What exactly do you mean by that, Mr Muller?'

'Cops,' I said flatly. 'Guys with big feet who have got a

solid relation with reality. We ought to tell them what's going on. We ought to recruit whatever help they can offer. In the meantime—'

'Oh, yes,' Dirk cut in at this juncture, his voice dripping with sarcasm. 'In the meantime! What will you be doing in the meantime, Mr Muller—sitting on your fanny and polishing your toenails, most likely?'

Whichever facet of his nature the guy showed you, you could be sure of one thing—it would be real surprising and fascinating.

I resisted the temptation to grab his two ears and beat his skull on the floor until he found the sense he was born with. Sandra Marsh might not like it a bit. All the same, it was Sandra's life at stake and I wouldn't have trusted Dirk with a hair from her head.

'I'll be trying to get to the bottom of the mystery,' I told him. 'Don't you think there is a mystery?'

'Oh, indeed I do, Mr Muller! The mystery is how you ever came to be recommended to Sandra in the first place. Police!' he spat with cold, concentrated contempt. 'Cops! You've been told what would happen if the police were brought in. Sandra's reputation would be trailed in the gutter, torn to shreds by the filthy-minded gossip-mongers. Sandra would be finished, ruined even!'

He paused there to get a breath and I poked a finger at what he was carrying around in lieu of a chest.

'Why don't you come out of your trance, Dirk,' I told him. 'Sandra finished? Sandra ruined? So what do you think will happen to her if some punk plants a .45 slug in the middle of her bosom? That won't finish her? That won't ruin her?'

A film of sweat oozed out on the actor's forehead.

'I've taken precautions,' he said defensively. 'I've hired two bodyguards. They watch her night and day.'

'Then howcome someone broke into her bedroom the other night?' I queried gently.

'I—I—' Dirk began. Then, 'There is no proof there was anyone in her bedroom. At least no one was found to be there.'

'So Sandra simply dreamed it out of her sleep? And what about the laugh she heard? Did nobody else hear it?'

The guy seemed reluctant to answer. At length he shook his head slowly from side to side. His eyes clung steadily to my face.

'So nobody did?' I coaxed.

'It appears that no one heard the laughter but Sandra herself.'

Dirk left me on that note, before I had the chance to ask him if he thought Sandra might be losing her grip.

I spent a quiet night in the guest bedroom in the east wing of the house. I woke early, rose and showered and shaved. Downstairs, I discovered that nobody else had risen yet. I was heading to the patio where the sunshine was already streaming down when a door opened and a sharp voice halted me in my tracks.

'Where are you going?'

I turned and said, 'Huh?' I was speaking to a skinny old bat of about fifty who regarded me with a pair of flinty grey eyes.

'You were going to sneak out there, weren't you?' she accused. 'You're called Paul Muller and you're some kind of detective. Well, just you watch how you go about it, buster. I don't care for guys who pad around like prowling tom-cats.'

'You mean you never go to bed?' I said. 'Never, never? You spend the whole night in your kitchen with your pots and pans, and your broomstick in the corner?'

'Like I just told you,' the biddy said coldly, 'watch how you go about it, buster.'

'I will, I will,' I promised. 'But what's cooking, gorgeous, besides that dark plot in your mind? Anything a hungry guy might eat before he outgrows his strength?'

'There's a hell of a lot more cooking than you'd ever guess, brighteyes,' the biddy said. 'And let's drop the gorgeous stuff, huh? If you're hungry come on in and take your chances. My name is Collins. My first name is Rachel. But don't expect me to tell you anything remotely resembling news, Muller. How would you go for toast, scrambled eggs and bacon?'

'Sounds swell, Rachel.' I took a chair by the kitchen table and watched her go about making the meal. I offered her a cigarette and she tucked it under her hair and behind her ear.

'Smoke it later,' she remarked casually. 'When are you going to solve the case?'

'I'm doing my best, Rachel. The fact is that I'm kind of short on information.'

'Oh,' she said. 'Information? In other words, you're one of these guys who keeps asking around instead of getting off your backside and digging under the rubbish pile. And boy, is there plenty of rubbish around at this minute!'

'Maybe you're referring to Sam and Jude?' I said as she dished out bacon and eggs and then reached for the coffee pot.

'Never mind what I'm referring to, Muller. You knock that chuck back and then go find whoever wants to kill Miss Marsh.'

'You figured it all out, Rachel? She is going to be killed?'

She shrugged and helped herself to a cup of coffee. She brought the cigarette from the back of her ear and lit it. She set herself down on a chair and looked at me.

'I've got this feeling,' she said ominously. 'It's hanging everywhere in the air ...'

'Yeah?' I said weakly. 'You've got second sight, maybe, Rachel?'

'A feeling,' she said stubbornly. 'You'd better get to work, Muller, and you'd better do it fast. It's death is what it is. Nothing but the smell of death!'

There's no point in saying how she ruined my appetite. At the same time I had a feeling of my own. The dame knew something or she was pretending to know something. Another thought struck me.

'Tell me, Rachel,' I said curiously, 'you've never been an actress yourself, have you?'

'You trying to be smart, Muller?' she said savagely. 'Because if you are, try doing it someplace else. Of course I'm not an actress. Who wants to be an actress? They're all a bunch of screwed-up kooks in my estimation. Now, eat every scrap of that breakfast and then take yourself the hell out of my kitchen.'

The house remained quiet when I left Rachel a short time later. I crept back upstairs and went along the passage to the west wing. I knew Sandra had her bedroom on this side, although I didn't know which bedroom it was. I found out when I saw the gross figure of Jude Tripp slumped on a chair directly in front of a bedroom door. Tripp was sound asleep, snoring lustily. I stood back and aimed a kick at the leg of the chair nearest to me. The leg didn't give but the result was enough to send Tripp springing up like a buffalo at bay.

'Oh, it's you, Muller,' he scowled sleepily when he had floundered around for half a minute. 'But why did you do that?'

'You're supposed to be on guard, chum,' I snarled at the guy. 'That means you stay awake. You know what used to happen to guys who fell asleep at their posts?'

A door opened across the way and Gale Bush peered out.

She was wearing a pink robe over a negligee that was so sheer it made me catch my breath.

'Cheese!' Jude said in amazement.

'Push your eyes back where they belong, pal,' I told him. 'Hi there, Gale,' I grinned, making a futile effort to banish a loving memory that popped straight into my mind.

'Is anything the matter, Paul?'

'Not much,' I said. 'Only this specimen was asleep when he should have been awake.'

'You're a liar,' Jude snorted. 'I was just sitting with my eyes closed.'

'Please, Paul,' Gale said pleadingly. 'Don't let's have a scene. Anyhow, Jude is Dirk's responsibility, is he not?'

'Suit yourselves,' I told her. 'But Dirk's going to have a whole lot to answer for if anything does happen to Sandra.'

I tore my eyes from the dame and went back down the stairs. I had reached the bottom step when I heard Dirk Williams speak my name. I looked up to see him standing at a bend in the staircase. He was wearing a deep crimson robe over bright blue pyjamas.

'Mr Muller,' he said icily, 'give me a moment of your time, if you please.'

I should have sensed a trap, and I did, but I walked blindly into it all the same.

'Sure, Dirk,' I said. 'What can I do for you?'

He told me what I could do for him. He spoke so softly and courteously he might have been telling me what a wonderful morning it was instead of advising me how I might make an interesting spectacle while disclocating my spine.

'And,' he added in the same charged manner, 'keep your nose out of my affairs. Jude and Sam are my affair. Protecting Sandra is my affair. Your business should be concerned with doing what Sandra paid you to do.'

'You know, Dirk,' I said evenly, 'I've got a hunch that Sandra can see nothing but the cute side of your nature. I've got another hunch that says she's going to be a disappointed gal one of these days. You don't have to act, chum; you're just naturally mean and pin-brained. And howcome she treats you like you were born with at least a couple of parts missing.'

I left him chewing it over. His obscenities followed me all of the way to the front door and lingered in my mind long after I'd driven away from the house of horrors.

Some thirty minutes later I brought the Jag to a halt opposite a dingy apartment building on Paris Avenue, Burville. I got out and entered a narrow hallway where eight or ten mailboxes were arrayed. Al Hoseck lived on the third floor and I climbed some creaky steps that finally gave on to the third landing. A scripted legend on Hoseck's door read, 'A. Hoseck—Artist'. I knuckle-rapped the door and put a cigarette between my lips while I waited. No answer. So Hoseck was another late riser in the mornings. I lit my cigarette and puffed for a few seconds, then rapped again. Still no answer. I tried the handle and the door opened. Here was a narrow, boxlike passage with another doorway leading into the apartment proper. The living room was a mess. It held three chairs, a couch, a table, a small bookcase with the books arranged on the shelves like somebody had stood at the wall opposite and thrown the books at it. A sweater was draped over one of the chairs, a jacket over another. There was an ashtray on the table with a mound of cigarette butts and dead matches in it. There was an overall odour as though the air in the place had been dead for a very long time.

'... How would it do if I took up this position, Al? Would it be better, do you think?'

'I like you best the way you are, honey. That's it. Don't move an inch.'

'Gee, Al, I can never get over your talent. How long is it going to take?'

'What's the hurry, honey? We've got all day, haven't we? Don't tell me you've lost your staying power, Cathy.'

'I've got as much as you have, Al. You should know that by this time.'

I began to come out in a cold sweat. I felt like a perverted eavesdropper at a kingsize orgy. The voices were drifting from the room beyond the living room, and I let my eyes wander into this direction. There was another door there and it was open ever so slightly. I tip-toed towards it and eased the door gently inwards.

The dame was stark naked. She was a sizzling redhead with a deep, deep bosom and the kind of hips I always keep thinking of as mature. She was reclining on a studio couch with her hair falling across her shoulders in a way that reminded me of a glorious sunset with the white clouds absorbing a lot of the sun's fire.

Al Hoseck was standing nearby, busily daubing paint at a canvas on an easel. He was a pretty tall guy, loosely built, with a shaggy mop of black hair curling about his ears.

The dame's eyes had been paying attention to Al, but now they saw me and widened. I gave her a warm grin and raised a finger to my lips. I might as well have screamed Geronimo for the way the redhead reacted.

She leaped off the couch and gave vent to a thin yell.

'Look, Al! Somebody is standing at the door, snooping. You didn't tell me you rented out your sittings to an audience!'

'Hi, folks,' I said heartily and went on into the room.

Cathy scrambled for her dress and began tugging it on over her head. When the material got snagged on her ample breasts she uttered a strangled moan.

'Of all the cheap, lousy tricks, Al Hoseck!'

'Hey, wait a minute,' Hoseck panted when he found his voice. 'What the hell is going on here?'

'You tell me,' Cathy stormed. She had won the battle of the bosom and snatched up her bra, panties and stockings. Then, with a horrified glare at me she sprang past me out of the studio and slammed the door behind her.

I figured Hoseck was going to swing one at me. He did brandish a rawboned fist for a split second, but then something must have planted a doubt in his head and he lowered the fist slowly. The outer door banged with a force that must have jarred the whole building. It jarred Al Hoseck for sure.

'Do you know what you have done, mister?' he gritted. 'Ruined the very last chance I had of having a real live model. How am I going to work if I don't have a real live model?'

'How about asking Sandra Marsh to come to your aid?' I suggested helpfully. 'I believe she's resting between shows at the minute.'

He had soft brown eyes that became hard, bitter orbs at the very mention of Sandra's name.

'Sandra Marsh!' he howled angrily. 'What do you know about Sandra? What are you doing here anyway? Oh, maybe I get the picture!' he went on with more restraint. 'She sent you here to strong-arm me into selling her those paintings. Well, you just go tell her they aren't for sale. Do you hear me, mister—they're not for sale.'

'Calm down,' I told him. 'I know you artistic guys are noted for your fiery temperaments, but there is a limit, pal.'

'Don't pal me,' he yammered. 'If you're not here to do a deal for the paintings, then why are you here? What's your name?'

'My name's Muller,' I told him. 'Paul Muller. If you'll lay

off pounding my hearing mechanism I might even let you have one of my cards. I'm a private detective, Al, pal. A gumshoe. A shamus. Sandra is in trouble at the moment, bad trouble—'

'Oh, yeah!' Hoseck sneered. 'I couldn't care less if she was in hades, mister. She did the dirty on me, the cheap little goddamn tramp—'

It was when I hit him. I couldn't remember two seconds afterwards how I'd done it. Reflex action, maybe. A yen to stuff something effective into the guy's big mouth, maybe. Anyhow, he took a tumble that upset his easel and brought the stretched, unfinished portrait of Cathy down on his head.

He sat on the floor for a while, a bemused look in his eyes while he fingered the angle of his left jaw. I took a seat on the couch and got a faint wiff of the fragrance Cathy had been wearing. Hoseck struggled upright and hung against the wall. He regarded the easel and the canvas before switching his shocked gaze to me.

'Rough stuff, eh?' he said bitterly. 'Well, two can play at that game, Muller. What kind of fit will you throw when you're locked up in a jail cell?'

'You don't like Sandra anymore, Al? Maybe you even hate her. Maybe you hate her bad enough to start a campaign of nasty phone calls that might send her out of her mind.'

'Campaign? Phone calls?'

He sounded surprised and his surprise sounded genuine. Still, if he was responsible for the threatening messages, he was hardly going to break down in tears and admit it.

'You mean you're not doing it, Al? I want an answer, chum, and I want a truthful answer. I've been hired to find this character and I'm not stopping until I do find him.'

The guy stroked his chin some more. He picked up the painting and laid it on a chair. He gathered up the easel and propped it against the wall. Then he turned towards the door.

'Where are you headed, Al?'

He didn't answer me. He went out and I followed him. In the living-room he plucked his jacket from the back of the chair and pulled it on. He went on outside and I went after him. He trod the passage to the landing, began to decend the stairs.

There was a phone in the ground-floor passage and he walked purposefully towards it. He halted, lifted the receiver and put his soft brown eyes on me.

'I'm giving you only one chance, mister,' he said in a gravelly voice. 'Take off and leave me alone or make yourself at home until the police arrive.'

'You wouldn't Al.'

He gave me an ugly smile and commenced dialling. I shrugged, touched him on the shoulder, then slugged him on the tip of his chin. I didn't wait to see him hit the deck. I left him and walked on out to the bright sunshine.

CHAPTER EIGHT

I halted the Jag close to the entrance of Sunrise Studios, got out and fitted my best smile into place. It was coming over real good, I figured, when I encountered the guy in the comic-opera uniform. He hardly glanced at me as I swaggered past him, then he brought me to heel with a lusty parade-ground yell.

'Hold it right there! Where do you think you're going? Somebody told you it was a public park?'

'Who, me?' I said in a hurt voice. 'But surely you recognise me, Colonel. It's odd that you don't when everybody else does. But maybe you just started working here yesterday?'

The guy had a hard gander at me and did something intriguing with his mouth. It twitched at the left corner and then the twitch jumped over to the other corner. All the while his light blue eyes assessed me from the feet up.

'No. I don't recognize you,' he said finally. 'I've been standing here for the last five years. The fact of the matter is I've never seen you before in the whole of my life. You got a pass?'

'You must be joking, Colonel. Here, have a look at my licence instead.'

I flashed my photostat, which didn't make any more impression than the cover of a cigarette pack.

'Private investigator? Now isn't that interesting. The fact of the matter is they've got their own security system here, Mr Muller.'

'Call me Paul,' I told him. 'You know, I'd like to hear more about the security system, Colonel.'

'Yeah, you would,' the guy said indifferently. 'Look, Mr Muller, put yourself into reverse and go find somebody else's gate to crash through, huh?'

He had it made, this lad. Five whole years. His boots were shined so you could see yourself in them. His uniform was spick and span. His chin and jowls were freshly shaved. And yet there was something about him that struck a false note—the feeling of superiority and power he had, maybe. Put some guys in a uniform and you do something terrible to their vanity.

'I'm real disappointed in you, Colonel,' I said regretfully. 'Didn't George tell you to expect me? Well, if he didn't, he should have done, and he'll eat his hat when he hears I was turned away.'

I sauntered back towards the gate and had gone three yards when the guy called after me.

'George who?'

'Goldman, of course.'

'Then you'd better come back here. The fact of the matter is there is Mr Goldman's car coming in now.'

There was a car swinging in, for sure. There was a chauffeur at the wheel of the sleek limousine and a hard-featured guy taking it easy in the back seat. The guy had to be George Goldman, but he just stared at me and through me, and the Colonel didn't miss one of the tricks.

'Wise guy, eh?' he growled. 'You know George and he'll eat his hat when he hears you were turned away?' he went on sneeringly. 'Okay, bud, keep drifting. Shoo! Shoo!'

I looked back and saw the limousine draw on to a parking area at the side of the sprawling buildings. George Goldman emerged and took the briefcase which the chauffeur held for him. I cupped my hands to my mouth and shouted.

'Mr Goldman!'

Goldman peered at me for a half minute before frowning and heading to a doorway in front of him. The guard in the comic-opera uniform began to close in on me threateningly.

'The fact of the matter is you're asking for it, bud.'

'Paul Muller, Mr Goldman!'

'Look, why don't you buy yourself a goddamn drum...'

'Take it easy, Colonel. The fact of the matter is that the dime has clicked. Have a look-see for yourself if you don't want to believe me.'

The dime *had* clicked. George Goldman was walking slowly into my direction now, rugged features alert, head tilted at a quizzical angle. He had the appearance of a prize fighter who had had too many fights and too few prizes. His dress was spruce and immaculate, though. 'Paul Muller, you say? You really are Paul Muller?'

'That's right, George,' I admitted modestly. 'The Colonel here will bear me out.'

'The Colonel? Oh, yes, I see! Ha, ha! well, shake hands, Muller and—' He made a brief pause and I could almost hear him finish by saying, 'come out fighting.' He didn't, though. He looked concerned and asked in a low voice, 'Has it to do with Sandra?'

'Yes, it has. I would like a few words with you, George, if you've got the time to spare.'

'Of course I've got the time to spare. Please come with me, Paul.'

I followed him into a long corridor that had panelled walls and a tiled floor. We finished up in a luxuriously appointed office that was all teak and marble and blondwood. Goldman gave me a cigar and a drink, then settled down on his own side of a beautifully polished desk. He placed his two elbows on the

desk and leaned forward expectantly, like he was waiting for a
bell to ring.

'Well, go right ahead, Paul,' he said in a taut voice. 'Don't
pull any punches. Just give it to me straight on the chin.'

I'd done enough mayhem for one morning, and anyhow I
figured Goldman might give me a better run for my money.
All the same, I felt so exasperated I could have hit the producer
on the head with a hammer had I been carrying one.

Why did everybody seem to resign themselves to the idea
that Sandra Marsh was a hopeless case and it was so inevitable that she was heading for some grisly showdown? Did
everybody—just like Al Hoseck—really believe the dame was
a hopeless case?

'She's had another phone call, George,' I told him.

'The dirty dog,' George said. 'I wish I could lay my hands
on him, Paul. Just for two whole minutes. Say, I was a boxer
one time, you know. Bet you never guessed.'

'I'd never have guessed in a hundred years. You'd make
mincemeat out of the guy, I take it?'

'I'd do more than that,' Goldman said with enthusiasm.
'Why, I remember that fight I had with Kid Frazee— Hey,
I'm not talking about a century ago, you understand! Just a
few years. Hell, I'm only thirty after all. Used to produce
amateur stuff on the side. Then one thing led to another...'

'Doesn't it always?' I said vaguely. 'Look, George, it isn't
as though I don't appreciate you reminiscing to me. I'm a
lover of most sports myself. But I got a business to keep going.
And thanks for getting me a client. To get back to this client—'

'Hell yes, Paul! Sandra. What did the phone call say this
time? Another of those stupid threats?'

'That's right,' I said. 'Another threat. But stupid? Well, I
wouldn't bet too heavily on it, George. This threat said the
curtain was all set to fall on Sandra's final act. I don't have

to spell out what it could actually mean.'

Goldman looked serious for a moment and his rugged face hardened into a tight, furious mask. Still, he seemed more puzzled than angry, I figured.

'But who would want to kill her, Paul?' he croaked. 'That's what I'd like to know.'

'I heard she used to be a popular sort of gal, George. Then I heard too she had developed a penchant for making enemies.'

Goldman leaped to Sandra's defence at once.

'Not deliberately, Paul. She isn't mean or petty, or anything of that nature. It's just what this racket does to you, especially if you're a woman. It makes you real tough, I guess, thick-skinned. Well, you don't get anyplace in this world except you've got a thick skin. Then there's the question of temperament. Dames are temperamental at the best of times. An actress who has fought her way to the top of the pile can afford to indulge herself.'

He hadn't said anything that didn't sound reasonable, but neither had he said anything that would provide me with the sort of clue I needed.

'You like her a lot, George?'

'Yeah, I do like her a lot,' he said aggressively. 'I don't want to see her hurt. I need her, Paul. I need her badly. She's resting between shows at the moment, but I want her to start rehearsing for a new series in two weeks from now. It's why I told her to hire you. I've heard plenty about you, Paul. Read some of your books. You struck me as the type of guy who might get to the bottom of the trouble—'

'You never thought of the cops?' I interrupted his back-slapping.

'Sure I thought of the cops. But that means talk, the wrong kind of publicity in the newspapers. Are you trying to tell me you find the assignment too much for you?'

'I've just got started,' I told him. 'I'm feeling my way. But I haven't got a crystal ball nor a magic wand, even. Are you in love with Sandra, George?'

He wasn't ready for the question, which was why I threw it at him just then. He sat back on his chair and burned me up a little for a few seconds. When he spoke again there was a thickness in his voice that warned me I was wandering on to quicksand.

'Yes, I do love her. I'd marry her tomorrow if she'd have me.'

'But she likes Dirk Williams too well to consider the idea?'

'Look here, Muller, you're deviating from the point,' the guy said sourly. 'What Sandra wants to do with her love-life is her own business.' He sat up straight again and put his elbows back on the desk. A dark suspicion had crossed his mind. 'Let's get one thing clear for openers. Was your purpose in coming here to get a wider picture of Sandra herself, or did you want to figure out if I might be jealous enough to do her physical harm?'

'Right on the button, George,' I said admiringly. 'No wonder you gave Kid Frazee such a wild time.'

'There's no sense in beating about the bush,' he rejoined with a weak smile. 'You got something to say, then come right out and say it.'

'Okay, George, I'll take your advice. Are you planning on setting up Sandra for a long fall?'

He didn't answer for the space of ten seconds. About half-way through them I got myself ready for the fist he was bundling together. He didn't throw the fist; instead the big fingers relaxed and he gave a harsh laugh.

'You're asking me if I'd murder Sandra?'

'Would you, George?'

'You know something, Paul,' he said sadly. 'I'm disappointed in you. 'You don't read like your books read at all. Maybe you do a little exaggerating when you get a typewriter in front of you, huh?'

'Maybe,' I agreed equably. 'But you still haven't answered my question, George.'

He slapped the desk so hard with his open hand the desk shivered in alarm.

'You're nuts, Muller. Plain raving nuts! Why should I kill Sandra, for Pete's sake? She's my one big star. I made her, mister. I grabbed her up the way you'd grab up a handful of clay and moulded her. Where do you think she'd have got without I was around to plot her course? Nowhere, that's where! So what happens if she drops down dead? I'll tell you what happens if she drops down dead. I lose the best meal ticket I ever had in my natural. Does all that answer your question?'

'It's a very good answer, I must admit, George.'

'Then cut out the crap, Paul, and don't act like you sent your brains on vacation and they lost their way home,' he said curtly.

'Maybe this guy doesn't really want to kill her,' I said, as if the thought had just occurred to me.

'Huh?' Goldman growled. 'What are you trying to spell out now? The threats say she's going to be killed, don't they?'

'And you actually believe what they say?'

'How the hell should I know?' he stormed. 'She hired you to investigate what is going on. But what's with the bright idea that struck you so suddenly?'

'It might be a gag, George—oh, a lousy mean gag without doubt. But it's possible the real motive behind the deal is to drive Sandra out of her mind.'

'As if I hadn't thought of it! Of course I've thought of it. She's half-way out of her mind at this minute.'

'You keep in touch with each other?'

'Yeah, we do. But not so close as you're trying to make out, if you see what I mean.'

I did see what he meant. I finished the dregs in my glass and pushed the glass aside. Goldman reached for the bottle but I shook my head I'd had enough.

'She told you about the laughter she heard, George? About the man who was supposed to be prowling in her bedroom?'

He nodded glumly. He had been playing with one of his cigars and now he clenched it between his teeth and lit it. He blinked through the cloud of smoke he blew.

'It could have been her imagination,' he said slowly. 'She told me no one else heard the laughter. There was nobody in her bedroom when one of Dirk's fat pups went to see what she was screaming about.'

'So you could be right, George, and she is in the process of losing her marbles one by one.'

He lunged to his feet abruptly and thumped on the desk some more. Just then he really did look like a pug who was straining to climb into a ring and do ten rounds with some-body.

'You're a private detective, Muller. From what I hear you're reckoned to be one of the very best in the business. Okay then! Shake the sand from your shoes. Do something positive. Do any damn thing so long as you catch this character and let me know who he is. I'll beat his head to a pulp. I'll break every bone in his miserable body. I'll—'

'How about Julia Dortmeyer, George?'

It hauled him up short with his mouth falling open.

'Julia Dortmeyer?' he echoed. 'All right, what about her?'

'She was opposition for Sandra, I believe. Around the time you were moulding Sandra from a handful of clay, Julia was right there all the time, waiting for the cue to come on.

You didn't bring her on. Julia didn't like it. Julia did some teeth-gnashing when you picked Sandra instead of her.'

'But Julia's a woman, for the love of Mike! You're saying she bears a grudge against Sandra? Well, go ahead and say it. It's true. But she isn't the only dame around here that can't bear Sandra's guts. Anyhow, Julia hasn't got the nerve to sell anybody a Kill Sandra Marsh campaign.'

'Where is she now?'

'She's resting,' Goldman said shortly.

'Meaning she's been stashed away someplace to bite her nails until you find her a part?'

'I'm not the only producer at Sunrise. I don't own the damn place.'

'But you can make or break an actress, George?'

'Maybe,' he said truculently. 'But, like I tell you, I'm only a producer. You're sniffing round the wrong tree.'

'Seems to me I'm going to have to sniff round plenty of trees before I find the one where the guy who throws his voice is hiding. Where does Julia live?'

'Lay off Julia, Muller.'

'Okay,' I shrugged. 'Play it close to the chest if you must, George. I'll have her address before five minutes have passed.'

'She lives at an apartment house on Jefferson Avenue,' Goldman scowled. 'But you'll be wasting time going to see her.'

'You haven't got anything else to contribute, George?'

It was evident that he hadn't. He showed signs of impatience and I shook his hand and left him.

It was a ten-minute drive from the studios to Jefferson Avenue. I hadn't asked the number of the apartment house where Julia Dortmeyer lived, but I found it with very little difficulty. The apartment house was a grey, disconsolate-looking dump that was about as far removed from the luxury of Hillview as two buildings can get.

There was no answer to my ring on the doorbell of number 26 on the second floor. I rang a couple more times, tried the doorhandle, then went downstairs and knocked on the manager's door. The manager was a fat, balding guy, who informed me he hadn't see Miss Dortmeyer in three whole days.

'The joint is busting at the seams with actors and actresses,' he told me. 'They come and they go. They hang around that Sunrise place like bees searching for honey. After a while they get discouraged and pull out.'

'So Miss Dortmeyer has pulled out?'

'I didn't say she had. She hasn't checked out and her things are still in her apartment. I looked no later than this morning. Say, she isn't in trouble, is she?' he added. 'One thing I don't want around here is the cops.'

'No cops,' I told him. 'I'm just a friend. I might call again later to look her up.

I went back to the street and sat in the Jag with a cigarette going. I sat there for a quarter of an hour, maybe, thinking of this and that. I was about to gun the motor to life when I noticed a Buick Skylark parked on the opposite side of the street. There was a guy at the wheel and he turned his head away quickly when he noticed I was watching him.

I stuck another cigarette between my lips, climbed out of the Jag and went across to the Buick. The guy was around twenty-five or so, dark and slick, but with a weak mouth and a receding chin. He was holding himself tensely and studied me with hawk-like readiness.

'Got a match, pal?'

'Sure,' he said, his breath gushing out of him in relief. He searched in a pocket and brought out a book of paper matches. 'Help yourself, buddy. I got more matches someplace.'

'Thanks a bunch,' I told him and lit my cigarette. I leaned

my elbow on the window frame and dribbled smoke into his eyes. He drew back, blinking and coughing.

'Hey, take it easy, buddy, will you!'

'Sure,' I said. 'Sorry. Waiting for someone?'

He had small rat's eyes and they ran around in their sockets like twin blobs of oil.

'Say,' he grated then. 'You a cop or something?'

'Just a friendly joe, buddy. Don't sweat all over your after-shave. Well, it's been nice meeting you, and thanks for the matches.'

I went back to my Jag and slid behind the wheel. When I looked at the Buick again it was taking off like it had a date with the moon. I kept looking in my rear-view mirror until the guy had cleared the street. Then I glanced at the match folder I was holding. It carried an ad. for an Anfield hotspot.

CHAPTER NINE

By the time I'd made a U-turn and driven to the end of the avenue there was no sign of the Buick. It was a pity I hadn't reacted a little sooner; but then, if I had, the driver of the Buick would have seen it all happening and made a counter-move to throw me off the scent.

Scent, I asked myself, what scent? Did the guy with the oil-blob eyes really fit into any slot in the drama? Could it not be, simply, he was just some nervous character who was ready to jump like a scalded cat on the minute that anybody spoke to him?

It was possible; I didn't think it probable. I had a strong hunch he had either been following me around Burville, or had been watching the front of Julia Dortmeyer's apartment building. If he had been watching the apartment then it seemed to indicate Julia's having some significance in the scheme of things. I didn't think it was the answer. The more I mulled it over, the more convinced I became that the guy's main aim had been to shadow me and keep track of my comings and goings.

I played his voice back against that of the punk who had knocked me cold in the beach-hut. They didn't match at all. Still, it didn't mean he hadn't been one of the beach-hut intruders. He could have been the one who restrained Alice while his pal was so busy knocking me around.

Okay, I told myself. Fine. But don't overlook something that sticks out about four miles. The uninvited beach-hut visitors had come primed with the knowledge that Sandra Marsh had hired me or was setting herself to hire me. It meant then they were in close contact with whoever was harassing Sandra. It also meant that somebody in Sandra's camp was connected with the effort.

George Goldman slid into my thoughts without conscious encouragement. After all, it had been Goldman's idea to hire me to solve Sandra's case. Was Goldman really the potential killer, and was he planning his moves like a chess-player, throwing out a lead here, a bluff there? If so, then he was going to be a real slippery eel to pin down.

I drew up at a drugstore and went in to use the phone. I rang Larry Stern's office in Anfield. Larry is an old buddy from way back and happens to be in my line of business. Of course it follows that we provide competition for each other, and we have been known to take a bite out of each other's neck occasionally. However, Larry has a bombshell of a secretary called Milly Wheeler, and it's Milly who gives us a neutral ground to manoeuvre in when our feelings towards each other happen to run high. Milly has an age-old yen to prove I'm really the man I purport to be, but so far I've never yielded to the many temptations she strews in my path. Well, if you start playing around with a guy's secretary, you really are asking for trouble.

It was Milly who answered my call.

'Yes?' she said in her most polite manner. 'Stern Investigations here. What can we do for you?'

'So business is bad, baby,' I said with a snigger. 'It's always bad when you polish up your Sunday go-to-meeting tone.'

'Paul Muller! of all the lousy tricks. Where have you been for the last ten years, Paul?'

'Knocking around,' I said airily.

'Don't tell me,' Milly retorted with an elaborate groan. 'From one perfumed pillow to another! And what's so wrong with the brand of perfume I use? But gee, Paul, it is good to hear your voice again. I was beginning to think you had really worn yourself to a shadow and had gone off to a monastery to recuperate.'

'Don't overestimate me, baby. I know I'm big stuff, but I've made a promise not to run out of steam until we jump on to that old choo-choo together.'

'That'll be the day, buster. That'll really be the day you get your chips. Did I say chips? What I meant to say was a set of crutches... But hold everything, Paul. The master himself has just come into the room. I'm sure you didn't ring us up just to get a weather report on the area. But what am I saying? Are you at home? Why couldn't you grace us with your person?'

'You know, baby, you're taking too many lessons from the canary. So how about sewing up your cute lips and putting Larry on the phone?'

Milly said something that made me wince. Then Larry Stern's voice was crackling in my ear.

'So you're at it again, witty boy,' he snarled. 'Why can't you lay off Milly and find somebody your own size?'

'All right, pal, I'll do that. In the meantime guess what. You're going to have the opportunity of doing me a big favour.'

'Is that so?' he said suspiciously. 'I don't like doing you favours, Muller. There's usually a string tied to its tail, and there's usually a can on the end of the string—'

'Okay, okay, bosom friend. Keep a little of your adrenaline for an emergency.'

'Then you aren't in trouble?' Larry said in a disappointed voice. 'I had visions of you hanging on to a cliff edge by your fingernails and wanting me to come and take you down.'

'Ha, ha! Very, very corny. I'm on a case, Larry. I want you to do a little something for me. And don't worry, you'll get paid for doing it. Pin your ears back and get a load of this licence number.' I recited the Buick's plate number and made sure he got it right.

'What do I do now?' Larry said bleakly. 'Decode the message?'

'You check it out with Vehicles Registration. When you do, you find out anything there is to know about the party who registered the heap. It's a green Buick Skylark. Then you relay the info. to me at this Burville number—'

'Burville? What are you doing in Burville?'

'Minding my own business, chum. Have we got a deal?'

'If the price is right. I can have a check run on the number of the car, but digging into the background of whoever owns the car could be something else. Aw, all right, Paul, I'll do what I can. What phone do you want me to call?'

I gave him the Hillview number.

'If I'm not there when you ring, don't leave any message,' I added. 'Keep trying until you strike oil.'

This Larry promised to do and hung up.

I got into the Jag and drove back to Hillview. I arrived just as the maid was serving lunch in the big dining-room. Petra was a dark, dusky-skinned maiden of about twenty-two or so. She gave me a big smile when I sat down at the table with Sandra, Gale, and Dirk Williams.

'Where do Jude and Sam eat?' I wondered when the maid had left and we started on the meal.

'In the kitchen,' Williams said grudgingly. 'I hope I don't have to repeat what I've already said to you, Mr Muller,' he added in a cold tone. 'Tripp and Walton are my sole responsibility.'

'You're welcome to them, Dirk,' I grinned. 'Well, folks, I

hope you all had a good morning in bed.'

Sandra didn't think the remark a bit funny. She was only nibbling at her food, I noticed. She was stretched out tighter than a drum-skin. Gale indulged in a short giggle and lowered her head when Williams bestowed a disapproving frown on her.

'We don't lie late abed as a rule,' Dirk explained frigidly. 'But of late we've been under such a strain that sleep has been practically impossible.'

'What Dirk is trying to say is that we feel a lot safer now that you're around, Paul,' the petite blonde contributed.

'I'm not trying to say anything of the sort, Gale,' Williams retorted constrainedly. 'In my opinion Jude and Sam can provide adequate protection if protection is necessary.'

'Then you haven't decided that it is?' I queried of the guy.

Instead of answering he glanced across the table at Sandra. Sandra was watching me with a gleam in her eye that told me she was displeased about something.

'What kind of a morning did you have, Paul?' she murmured.

'So-so,' I said. 'Look—what's with the air of gloom? You're all about as cheerful as a gathering at the morgue. There wasn't another phone call while I was out, was there?'

'Not the kind you mean,' Sandra replied in a detached manner. 'But there was a phone call—'

'Not just one,' Dirk Williams snapped heatedly. 'But two of them. Oh, why don't you have it out with him here and now, Sandra?'

'Yes do,' Gale cried excitedly. 'Paul is right, you know. What we all need is to be cheered up. A row, a fight. Anything to break this damn boredom...'

'Gale!' Sandra said tautly. 'How can you be so heartless, so utterly cruel?'

'Forgive me, honey,' Gale groaned and slipped from her chair to dash round me to Sandra. She put her arm about Sandra's shoulder and laid her cheek comfortingly against hers. 'Yes, I am heartless. I am cruel. I'm a cruel, heartless bitch. Call me a heartless bitch, darling! And on top of everything you've done for me!'

It had all the overtones of a crummy third-rate melodrama, and I choked on the food I was swallowing. I looked at Dirk to see what his reactions were and found him regarding me like I was the lead in a horror film and had callously blundered on to the wrong set.

'Don't rush off,' Gale was saying now. 'You mustn't allow it to annoy you, honey. You haven't eaten a bite, hardly...'

'Just leave me alone, Gale,' Sandra panted and continued getting up from the table. She went on to the door of the room, halted and stared back at me. 'I'd like to see you in the lounge, Mr Muller. Directly you have finished your meal.'

I didn't answer her. I just studied the door after she had banged it closed on herself. Dirk Williams began making queer noises in his throat.

'It's all a terrible mistake,' he mused regretfully. 'If only she'd left me to handle it, everything would have turned out right in the end.'

I didn't answer Dirk either. Not that he was actually talking to me. He appeared to be talking to himself. He flung down his napkin and started for the other door—the one leading into the hall. He opened it and passed out and I was left alone in the dining-room with Gale Bush.

She resumed her chair and had another giggle to herself. She giggled until tears stood in her eyes and I figured she was going to take off on a flight of hysterics.

'All right, baby,' I said sourly and flung my knife and fork on my plate. 'I'll buy it. What the hell is the matter with

everyone in this house? What did I say? What did I do? I've
seen more manners in a pigpen at a meal hour.'

'It's Al Hoseck,' Gale bubbled between waves of mirth. 'He
rang up Sandra and threatened to sue her.'

'He did, did he? Well, he seemed to be capable of it right
enough. But what did Sandra do to Hoseck?'

'It isn't what Sandra did to him, Paul; it's what you did to
him. He claims you chased off his model, practically wrecked
his studio, then broke about six teeth in his mouth.'

'Is that all? Gee, and I thought I'd made a proper job of
busting the guy's jaw!'

'But you can't behave in this way, Paul,' Gale urged when
she had calmed a little. 'I mean, you're going to cause the
very thing that everybody's trying to avoid. Publicity, and
bad publicity at that. If Al takes it into his head to make a
complaint to the police, then Sandra's goose is cooked.'

'Why aren't you crying your eyes out as well? Or can it be
that you've got the only sense of humour there is around here?'

'Cry? I've had enough of crying. I need a slice of fun for
a change. And boy, can you provide the fun, Paul!'

'Listen, baby. Turn if off. I thought you wanted to act discreet. But Dirk mentioned two phone calls. What was the
other one in aid of?'

'It was George Goldman,' the dame told me. 'I didn't hear
what he said to Gale. She told Dirk, I believe, but they all
clammed shut on me when I got curious.'

I kicked my chair back and stood up. Gale wanted to know
where I was going and I said I was going to see Sandra.
Gale came over to stand in front of me, her small, firm breasts
jutting in provocative promise. There was a tracery of moisture
on her lips.

'Don't be too hard on her, Paul,' she pleaded. 'She certainly
is getting a rough time.'

'Do you really like her as much as you pretend to, lotus blossom?'

'What! What a dreadful thing to say. Of course I like her. I care for her. We're sisters, practically. I don't know what she would do without me.'

'And I bet you don't know either what you would do without her.'

Her hand flashed to my face but I trapped the wrist before she could land the blow, then I pulled her to me and kissed her hard on the mouth.

'Slow down, baby, will you? My methods might not be exactly orthodox, but I've got plenty of results that must do something for a cynic.'

'So long as you keep those nasty cracks under cover,' she panted. 'And don't kiss me until I tell you to kiss me. We might have started some kind of fire, but this isn't the ideal setting for a furnace.'

'I'll remember that, beautiful. And keep the old flag flying, huh?'

'Never say die, Paul,' she gurgled. 'I won't.'

I found Sandra waiting impatiently in the lounge. She had been striding up and down on the lush carpet, puffing at a cigarette, and she swung round to face me immediately I entered. She didn't waste time in getting to the point.

'You've done a terribly stupid thing, Paul,' was her opening shot. 'Are you completely crazy to go to Al Hoseck and beat him around until you almost half-killed him?'

'Al told you I did that? Well, if he did Sandra honey, the guy is a double-barrelled liar. I merely—'

'Enough!' she interrupted me in a shrill voice. 'Whatever Al is he isn't a liar.'

'But he hates you, Sandra. He said so himself. What do

you suppose I hit him for, anyhow—because the jerk didn't like the colour of my eyes? He called you a tramp, baby doll, and not only that: he said you were cheap—'

'Al said that about me?' she moaned. 'But he couldn't. He wouldn't!'

'So you're paying me to tell a pack of lies?' I grated. 'Isn't that it, Sandra? You're calling *me* a liar. Okay, go ahead and call me a liar. But on the very minute you do I'm going to take off from this crazy house and never even think of it again.'

'No, no, Paul! You can't do that. All right, I do believe you. Al was angry. I've given him good cause to be angry. I can't altogether blame him. But please rid your mind of the notion that Al would do anything to harm me. I know he wouldn't.'

'You don't know one damn silly thing,' I snarled at her. 'And look who's calling the pot black, for Pete's sake! You accuse me of telling lies. What about your own self and your complete disregard for the truth, honey? You led me to believe you might have one or two enemies. One or two! From what I've dug up this far you're a very lucky gal to have one friend in the entire wide world.'

'But, but...' she wailed. 'I don't understand.'

'Then it's high time you did understand,' I said bitingly. '*Where?* might have elevated you away up in the charts with the people who view you from a distance, but it didn't do your ego any good. It made you selfish in the eyes of the folk you used to rub shoulders with. It gave you ideas about your place in the roll of immortals. Well, take a tip from somebody who's seen life from just about every vantage point there is, honey. Whatever else you think about yourself, you're human, you're involved with the herd, whether you like it or not...'

'Stop it, Paul. Stop it!'

'I won't stop it,' I went on ruthlessly. 'You hired me, Sandra. You've paid me five grand for straightening out your affairs.

That's a hunk of money in anybody's language, and the least I can do in return is show you that you don't have one enemy who would enjoy putting flowers on your tombstone. You've got a dozen at least. Maybe more for all I know.'

'Get out of here!' she screamed. 'Get out before I tear you to pieces with my bare hands!'

She wasn't even kidding. She socked me like she'd socked me in the bedroom of the Hotel Rialto. She hit me twice and then crumpled up in a heap on the floor.

I stood looking at her for a half-minute. Her shoulders shook and her hair tumbled over them in a silken stream. Then I left her and headed for the door.

Her thin cry came after me.

'Paul . . . Wait!'

'Yeah?' I said stonily. 'Wait for what—for you to get your strength back so you can give me a proper working over?'

'I'm sorry, Paul. Please forgive me. You can't go off and leave me like this.'

'Don't bet your last buck on it. Sandra.'

I looked at the door and then I looked at the dame again. My big heart won. I went to her and helped her to her feet. She seemed to have need of support so I put my arm about her waist.

'Oh, Paul,' she whispered, turning her head into my shoulder. 'Please don't leave me. Please stay and do what you can for me. Yes, it's true that I don't have many friends. I need a friend, a friend I can lean on for support.'

I figured I was supporting her fine, but in case she wanted the full treatment I put both arms around her. She was soft and pliable just then, and she was playing hob with my hormones.

We were really melting towards each other when two things happened simultaneously. The door of the lounge opened and

Dirk walked in, and the phone on the oak-topped table rang.

Sandra broke our clinch and rushed to the phone while Dirk Williams studied me like I was the king of two-timing skunks.

'Yes!' Sandra said hoarsely. 'Sandra Marsh speaking. Who—'

She stopped talking and gave a cry of pure terror. I dashed over and caught the mouthpiece as it slipped from her lifeless fingers, then held the instrument to my ear.

'... So don't forget, Miss Marsh. Your number has just come up. Goodbye for now, sweetheart.'

The voice went away. There was a sharp, decisive click. I wheeled round in time to see Dirk Williams catch the dame before she fell.

The voice I'd heard belonged to the guy who had softened me up at White Surf Bay.

CHAPTER TEN

Night fell as night must.

I got back to Hillview around midnight and left the Jag on the parking strip. I felt so bushed I didn't want to do anything but crawl into bed. I'd spent the afternoon and evening in checking up on more of Sandra's acquaintances. It had been abortive effort and had taken me nowhere.

'I'd gone back to the apartment house where Julia Dortmeyer was supposed to be staying and had slipped the manager a five-spot to let me see her apartment with my own eyes. I didn't find her body in a sack and stuffed into the closet; I did find a few of her personal belongings—enough evidence to indicate it hadn't been her intention to stay away permanently when she'd left.

Now it was around midnight, like I said. The air was cool— a lot cooler up here in the hills than in Burville—and the sky was a wide girdle of twinkling stars. I locked up the Jag and headed for the front door of the house. The house was in darkness and I didn't have a key to let myself in. It seemed that everybody here went to bed early and stayed there until late the next morning. I tapped gently and was admitted almost immediately by Hackett. He hovered there in the shadows and sent a shiver running over my spine until he switched on the hall light.

'Glad to see you back, Mr Muller,' he said politely. 'Had a nice evening, I hope?'

I looked at him just to make sure he wasn't breaking one of the rules at Hillview and being funny, but he was quite sober and I said it hadn't been such a good evening at all.

'Where is Dirk?' I added. 'Gone to bed like everyone else in the joint?'

'I haven't gone to bed, Mr Muller,' a cold voice said from

the depths of the hall. 'In spite of what you might think of that last telephone call, I am inclined to treat it with the utmost gravity.'

'No kidding?' I murmured. 'But I figured you had hired Jude and Sam to fend off the uninvited. Do you think that you're over-working them, maybe?'

'They're both on guard tonight,' he announced and came on along the hall to the bottom of the staircase.

'Swell, Dirk. Then I can sleep like a baby myself and not have a thing to worry about. But howcome I didn't see them? If you post a guard, isn't the obvious place to post it outside of the house?'

His dark eyes flickered in annoyance.

'Really, Mr Muller. I'm not entirely stupid. Of course the outside of the house is covered. Sam is outside and Jude is inside. Jude is stationed at Sandra's bedroom door. He has orders to shoot anyone who attempts an entry. *Anyone*, Mr Muller,' he stressed sneeringly. 'I trust therefore that you don't walk in your sleep.'

He was hitting me below the belt but I let it ride. I asked him how Sandra had got through the remainder of the day.

'Not too well,' he replied accusingly. 'The threat continues to hang over her. Nothing seems to have altered since we hired you, Mr Muller. It was necessary to give Sandra more sedatives to keep her calm.'

'It isn't sedatives Sandra needs, pal; she needs real protection. The sort of protection that only the police can give her.'

He gnawed at his underlip in an agony of vexation.

'Making such a decision isn't within your scope, Muller. Do try to remember it.'

I left him and went on up the stairs. At the first bend I paused to glance down at him. He was standing there, staring up at me, his mouth curled contemptuously now.

I looked along the corridor leading to the west wing and saw Jude Tripp slumped on a chair opposite Sandra's bedroom door. Tripp gave me a wan grin and lifted his hand in a half-hearted salute.

'Hi, Sherlock,' he smirked. 'Make sure you lock your door tonight. Dirk has a hunch that somebody could have his throat cut come morning.'

'You'd better stay awake yourself then, Jude honey. With Dirk so nervous like this he might run amok himself. You've got the sort of shape a guy might easily mistake for a pin-cushion.'

I entered my room and did as fatso said and locked the door. Then I peeled off my clothes and had a shower, after which I donned a set of kinky pyjamas and rolled into bed.

I fell asleep at once.

I came awake with someone tapping gently on my door.

I sat up in bed and listened until the tapping was repeated. Then I hit the floor and went over to the door to open it.

Gale Bush stood there, clad in baby-doll pyjamas, her eyes large and glistening fearfully. Her breathing was shallow.

'Paul, I'm frightened as hell,' she confessed frankly. 'I've got the feeling that something awful is going to happen to-night.'

'What do you mean, tonight?' I scowled, glancing at my strap-watch. 'It's two o'clock, sweetie-pie, and that says it's morning. Anyhow, what do you want me to do? You said we must be discreet. You said—'

'I know what I said,' she interrupted and brushed past me into the room. 'Can't we sit and talk for a while or—or some-thing?' she added when I continued to stand by the open door.

'And run the risk of Sandra's wrath? Not to mention what Dirk might dream up to hit me with?'

Her chuckle had a hard core to it.

'You're not afraid of Dirk, are you?'

'Of course I'm not afraid of Dirk. Well, no more than I'd be afraid of a rattlesnake. Didn't you pass Jude on your way here?'

'Yes, I did. But he's sound asleep. I can't get over how he can sleep sitting upright in that chair.'

'And Dirk claims he's giving Sandra protection!'

'Don't get into a sweat about it, Paul. I'm a very light sleeper myself. If somebody did try to force his way into Sandra's room I would hear the commotion at once.'

'Who says the killer is going to make a commotion?' I said.

Gale shuddered and clutched my arm. Her eyes had a frantic glitter in them now.

'A killer! Then you think there really is a killer waiting for his chance to get at Sandra?'

'*I* think so? Doesn't everybody think so? I'm not a clairvoyant. I'm just a plain little down-to-earth gumshoe.'

'Little, he says!'

By this time Gale had me in some kind of clinch. I tried to beat her off. She wanted to close the door. I wanted the door to stay open.

'Oh, all right, baby,' I said resignedly at last. 'You win. But don't blame me if the whole dump is buzzing with gossip, come the dawn.'

'Let tomorrow take care of itself, I always say, darling.'

She had partly discarded the top of her pyjamas when there was a crisp rap on the door. Gale froze for an instant, then uttered a low groan and broke away from me.

'Who can it be, Paul?' she whispered in a stricken voice.

'Who else but Dirk,' I gritted. 'That guy has got ants in his pants tonight. I turned towards the door but Gale clawed at my arm to hold me back.

'Are you stone crazy?' she panted. 'You can't let him in here. Why, he'd tell Sandra and then there would be hell to pay...'

'I don't intend to let him in.'

I went on over to the door as it took another crisp thumping.

'Mr Muller, are you there?' Dirk Williams demanded.

'Sure, I'm here. What's the big idea rousing a guy from his sleep? Is anything the matter?'

He didn't answer for a moment, then, 'Gale is absent from her room. I can't find her.' His voice dripped with suspicion.

'Huh?' I grunted and opened the door a fraction. Williams would have pushed himself into the room if I hadn't placed a restraining hand against his chest. 'Sorry, Dirk, a man's bedroom is his castle, I always say. You surely don't think Gale would have wandered in here?'

'Where can she be then?' he bleated. 'She knows the danger of wandering around after darkness.

'Yeah, you'd think she should, wouldn't you. But you take it up with her, pal, and leave me out of it.'

'Could—could I come in for a few minutes, Mr Muller?' he said craftily. 'I'm really at my wits' end tonight.'

'Me too,' I told him. 'But not tonight, handsome. Why don't you settle for a cold shower, and maybe you'll feel cooler afterwards?'

'You filthy-minded bastard,' he said thickly and went off in a black huff.

I closed the door and locked it. Gale had decided to have a hearty giggle to herself. I stood there and scowled at her.

'You figure it's funny, don't you,' I growled. 'Well, go right ahead and have your hysterics. But consider one aspect of this with your tiny mind, baby. Besides having ants in his pants, Dirk has now got a bee in his hat. It says you're in here, and it also says you've a million-to-one chance of getting back to your room without being spotted by him. Then what? Somebody around here is going to get himself branded as a nineteen carat sex-maniac.'

'You're so right, Paul,' she said soberly. 'I can't slip out without Dirk seeing me. But don't you realise what it all means—I'm going to have to spend the rest of the night right here in your room.'

'That might be your interpretation of the gag, honey, but I've got another one that says you're getting the hell out of here within the next five seconds. I've got a reputation to think of, for Pete's sake.'

'Don't we all?' she said recklessly.

'Maybe. But I happen to trade with mine. So do you walk out on your two feet, or do I have to carry you?'

'You wouldn't, Paul!'

'Darn tootin' I would, and I am.'

'I'm going to scream,' she shrilled when I approached her.

'Yeah, you just scream, moonflower. Then, tomorrow, we'll see about rigging up some chains to clank. In a day or so we'll have hit on the right atmosphere for the joint.'

'Don't put your hands on me, Paul!'

'Aw, come off, it, Gale. Enough is enough.'

I grabbed her up and slung her across my left shoulder. Gale beat on the small of my back and hissed a stream of colourful abuse. I took her to the bedroom door.

'I'm going to scream, Paul. Really I am! I'm going to scream and scream, and then, when Dirk happens on the scene, do you know what?'

'I'll buy it,' I said curiously, pausing.

'I'll tell him you tried to rape me. No,' she amended quickly, 'I've got a better idea! I'll tell him you've already raped me.'

'You wouldn't.' Cold sweat rippled out all over me.

'Okay, plain little down-to-earth gumshoe, just open the door and let me get into my act. If you think Sandra can deliver some lines that a guy scripts for her, then wait until you hear the way I can deliver an effort of my own.'

She had me buffaloed. I pulled her off my shoulder and let her fall on the floor. She sat there and rubbed her left hip ruefully.

'Why did you do that?' she said with an angry sob.

'Because you win, honey,' I said wearily. 'And just remember it's a very small bed.'

'So what?' she said, pulling herself together and smiling happily. 'I'm a very small gal, if you've never noticed.'

I knew it was a scream that brought me awake, but I wasn't sure whether it had happened in a dream I was having, or if Gale had made up her mind to sell me out after all. By the time I sat up in bed the dame was already sitting up beside me. She was trembling violently and had one of her hands stuffed half-way down her throat.

'What was that, Paul?' she cried hoarsely. 'Did you hear it?'

'Sure I heard it. You mean it wasn't you?'

'Of course it wasn't me. I—'

It came again, a thin, high-pitched cry of pure terror that sent ice-water dashing along my spine.

'It's Sandra, Paul! Something must be happening ... Oh, don't leave me, Paul,' she croaked as I sprang out of bed and grabbed my robe from the back of a chair.

I pulled on the robe and hurried from the room, sprinting along the passage that led to the west wing and the bedroom where Sandra Marsh was in the throes of whatever desperation was harassing her. I bumped into Dirk Williams coming from the opposite direction, flung the guy aside, and raced through the open bedroom door.

Sandra was lying across her bed, half on it and half off it. Jude Tripp stood helplessly in the middle of the floor, a bemused expression on his heavy-jowled face.

'I didn't see anything,' he babbled stupidly. 'I didn't hear anything, even...'

Sandra seemed to have fainted and Dirk started in to slap her cheeks. The dame groaned and rolled over and opened her eyes. They stared in horror. She would have sprang from the bed had Williams not restrained her.

'Don't move, sweetheart. Take it easy. Stay where you are.'

Sandra was still struggling with Williams as Gale entered. She told Dirk to leave Sandra alone and straightaway the TV star threw herself into the blonde's arms.

'There, there, honey,' Gale crooned comfortingly. 'It's all right now. I'm here and no one is going to touch you.'

'It—it was horrible, Gale—'

'What was?' I asked gently. 'Did you have another phone message?'

Sandra shook her head from side to side. She didn't answer me. She laid her head on Gale's shoulder and her whole body trembled violently. If this went on she would soon have a honey of a breakdown.

'Please get her a drink, Dirk,' Gale requested. 'A stiff one.'

Williams stared at the blonde for a moment, a peculiar light glinting in his eye. He swung to me and let me have the same treatment momentarily, then he spun on his heel and left the room.

I took Jude's arm and led him from the bed. Out in the passage Williams was remonstrating with a near-hysterical Collins and the chattering Petra.

'Look, calm down, will you,' he pleaded with them. 'Nobody has harmed Miss Marsh. Nobody broke into her room. Nobody is prowling in the house. She simply had a nightmare.'

The guy had it all off pat and it was good to see that somebody was definite about something.

'You're hurting my arm,' Jude grunted.

'Maybe you need to have it broken,' I snarled at him. 'Then you might stay awake when you're supposed to be awake.'

'But I was awake, Mr Muller. Honest, I was. I didn't see a thing. I didn't hear a thing.'

'Nothing?'

'I told you. Nothing.'

I left him and looked around the room. The windows were closed and fastened. There was nobody in the closet, nobody under the bed. So Dirk Williams was right and Sandra *had* been having a nightmare?

Williams returned with a drink and was offering it to Sandra when Gale took the glass from him and held it to the distracted girl's lips.

'If everybody would leave now,' she said. 'Yes, you too, Dirk. I can handle Sandra.'

'I want to hear what happened,' the guy declared stubbornly.

'I thought you already knew what happened,' I butted in. 'You said Sandra had had a nightmare. Do you mean you were just fooling all of us?'

He flung me a glare of distilled venom.

'Please go away, Mr Muller. You won't be missed if you do. So far you haven't done one single, solitary thing to throw light on the trouble. Indeed, you have merely brought further trouble on us.'

'Like to make a small bet on it?'

'Oh, do stop bickering like a couple of juveniles,' Gale cried waspishly.

Surprisingly, it was Sandra herself who resolved the matter. She had knocked back three-quarters of the contents of the glass and now sat up on the side of the bed. Apparently she had gained partial control of her faculties. She raised a hand.

'All of you please go away, with the exception of Mr Muller. I wish to talk with him.'

'Now look,' Williams blustered, 'isn't it plain that Muller is nothing better than an ineffectual bungler? If you'd only listened to reason at the beginning—'

'She did listen to you, buster,' I told the punk. 'And what does she have to show for it? Why don't you do what she says and take a powder?'

A moment later the door closed and I was alone with Sandra.

'Okay, baby,' I coaxed. 'Dirk says it was a nightmare. Was it a nightmare, and if so, what did you dream about?'

'No, Paul,' she began hoarsely. 'It wasn't a nightmare. I was sound asleep when it brought me awake. A voice ... It was a voice. It spoke in a sort of high-pitched whisper. It—it seemed to fill the whole room.'

She paused to take a cigarette from a box on the bedside table. Her fingers trembled so badly she could hardly cope. I lifted the lighter that was there too and flicked it on for her. She puffed hungrily for a few seconds, her green, hazel-flecked eyes scanning my face anxiously.

She said pleadingly, 'You do believe me, Paul, don't you? You must believe me! I can see that none of the others do—Dirk nor Gale nor anybody else.'

'I'm keeping a wide-open mind,' I said carefully. 'Tell me what you thought the voice said.'

'Thought it said!'

'Sure, honey,' I coaxed. 'You admit it awakened you from your sleep. I've never met anyone who could swear to having crystal-clear comprehension on the moment of awakening.'

The argument appeared to soothe her, but not much.

'It—it said, "The time is drawing close, Miss Marsh." That was all. It kept repeating it over and over again, like a phonograph record. I thought I was going crazy. But maybe I am going crazy!'

She gripped my arm and her fingers dug through the sleeve of my robe. Then she released the grip slowly, finger by finger, her eyes never leaving my face.

'That's better,' I said and grinned. 'Relax. It comes easy once you get the hang of it.'

'Don't treat me like an infant, Paul. I've had enough babying to do me for the rest of my natural. Just tell me if you think I really am going crazy.'

My grin weakened to a feeble smile.

'Of course you're not going crazy. You look sane enough to me, Sandra. So let's try and get it straight. You were sound asleep. This whisper brought you awake. You didn't hear anything before that? I mean, it actually was the voice you heard first of all and not—'

'No!' she panted, remembering. 'There was some kind of sound—like paper being rustled, or wood burning. A crackling. I'm sure I heard that—'

'Crackling?'

'Where are you going, Paul?' she cried when I lunged from my chair.

I told her to keep calm and I wasn't going anywhere special. She remained silent and watchful while I began another search of the room, a more thorough search this time. She must have thought I was going nuts myself, and maybe I was.

It took five minutes to strike oil—or more accurately, the instrument that had been used to frighten the daylights out of Sandra. I found it planted on the top window ledge, out of range of anything but the closest examination. It was a tiny radio receiver.

CHAPTER ELEVEN

Sandra stared blankly at what I held in my hand. When I made no reply to the questions she fired at me she came over to see what it was that had fascinated me.

'Paul,' she cried then, 'it isn't some kind of bomb?'

'You could call it a bomb and be on the safe side, honey. Sure you can't guess exactly what it is?'

She stretched out a finger to touch the receiver. When she did touch it she withdrew the finger as though it had touched fire.

'It's a radio of some description!'

'You've gone and hit it on the head,' I complimented her. 'So now you know you weren't having nightmares, and now you know too that you aren't going crazy.'

She gave a short laugh that threatened to become a deluge of tears. Then she clapped her hands together in little-girl glee.

'Oh, I could kiss you, Paul! You've put a lot of my fears at rest. That laughter I heard. The voices ... But just how does it operate?'

'It operates simply. This is planted in your bedroom, and then whoever wants to pass a message along to you stands outside someplace and talks into the transmitter.'

Sandra's eyes were a study in blatant horror.

'How perfectly diabolical, Paul! Why, if you hadn't found it I might have been driven out of my mind. I—' She stopped speaking when another thought occurred to her. I knew what she was going to say, but I let her go ahead and say it all the same.

'Who could be at the back of it, Paul?'

'That's what we've got to find out, baby,' I said. I took one of her cigarettes and lit it. She was starting for the bedroom door when I told her to hold it and asked her where she was thinking of going.

'I want to tell Dirk and Gale. I want to show them how wrong they've been. Oh, they heard the phone calls for themselves, of course. But they never believed what I said about the laughter I heard, and the man who came into my room.'

'So okay, Sandra. They didn't believe you when you badly needed someone to believe you. So we won't tell them about this—for a little while at any rate. We'll keep it a secret between our own two selves. But remember, this doesn't explain the man in your room.'

She paused and thought it over for a moment. It was plain she was tempted to disagree with me. Finally she inclined her head reluctantly.

'All right, Paul. Still, if you have the notion that Dirk or Gale would talk about it outside of the house, you're wrong.'

'I'm not suggesting they would talk, honey, but why risk having such a possibility?'

'What are you going to do with the receiver? I know what I'd like to do with it—put it beneath a hammer and smash it into a million damn pieces.'

She nearly had a fit when I returned to the window ledge and put the instrument back in the spot where I'd found it.

'What are you doing—making it easier for whoever is planning to kill me?' she hustled.

'Now see here, Sandra,' I said roughly, 'I'm in charge of your problem or I'm not. If I'm to succeed in what you're paying me to do, then I must have a free hand. We've found out that the voices and whisperings you heard didn't happen in your head. They happened someplace beyond the walls of this house, but not too far away. Also, there's another interesting item we mustn't overlook.'

'What?' she asked tensely.

I pointed at the window ledge. 'It didn't fly in and take roost there under its own power. Somebody had to put it there. Move it and you frighten off this character. Talk about it and eventually the news will reach his ears.'

She went back to the bed and sagged down on the edge of it. She began to tremble and her cheeks turned a ghastly grey pallor.

'Who—who could have done it, Paul? Who could have gotten into the house and into my bedroom—' She broke off there and an agonised groan was torn from her throat. 'Oh, no, it can't be! It couldn't be! I refuse to believe it...'

'A member of your own household?' I nudged gently.

Her eyes flashed on me accusingly. Her hands clenched tightly.

'You're saying it was?' she panted thinly.

'No, honey, I'm not. I'm not saying a thing until I get to the bottom of it.'

The door of the bedroom was rapped and Dirk Williams' harsh voice filtered through.

'What the hell's going on in there?' he snarled impatiently.

I walked over to the door and gripped the handle. I held it against Dirk's frantic efforts and eyed the dame steadily.

'You'll keep quiet, Sandra?'

'Yes, yes, I will! But please hurry and discover who it is, Paul. I've the feeling there isn't much more time left.'

Both Williams and Gale were outside the door when I opened it. They stared curiously when I walked out and headed along the passage to my own room. There was no sign of

Jude and I wondered where he was. The heck with the whole caboodle, I thought. There was hanky-panky going on inside these four walls for sure.

I pulled off my robe and pyjamas, dressing swiftly and pushing my spare .38 inside the waistband of my pants. I went to the door and looked up and down the passage. There was nobody in evidence, so I started for the stairs. The hall below was a well of darkness, which suited me fine.

At the bottom I got entangled with a lot of skinny limbs and plenty of tough muscle. It was wrapped up in the form of Rachel Collins who cursed heartily for a half minute until she realized who she was grappling with.

'So it's only you, Muller,' she grated in disgust. 'I might have expected it.'

'What were you really expecting, gorgeous?' I growled. 'Buck Rogers in person? Or would you settle for a guy with a wild gleam in his eye and a cleaver in his hand?'

'You pick a swell time to make cracks, Muller,' the biddy griped. 'I'm getting ready to take off through that door on the second Miss Marsh screams again. I've had a bellyful, and it's all a sane woman can take. Where are you going?' she asked when I went on to the front door.

'To take a walk in the fresh air. Like to join me in the bright moonlight?'

'You're nuts,' she scowled. 'Everybody around here is going nuts. If you've any sense left in your head, Muller, you'll get in your heap and take off.'

Good advice, I figured, releasing the bolts and drawing the door to without closing it when I passed out. There was something real nasty hanging over Hillview, and I didn't mean the dark clouds that were trying to blot out the sliver of moon riding in the sky.

I had bypassed the asphalt forecourt and had reached the

east corner of the house when a voice lanced towards me from the shadows.

'Stick 'em up!'

It was Sam Walton, gun in hand, who had emerged from the border of shrubbery. I said nothing until he came close enough to recognize me.

'Hi there, Sam. Put your gun away and get back to your post, pal. It's only me.'

'Yeah, I figured it was you, Muller. What's all the fuss about inside?'

'Miss Marsh thinks someone was talking to her.'

'Not again! Say, there's one dame that's really heading for the bugpen. So you're going to tuck your tail down and pull out, shamus? Well, I hardly blame you.'

'Nobody's pulling out, chum. I'm going to have a mosey through the grounds.'

'Yeah? Picking daisies, maybe? There's nobody in the grounds. I've been watching the driveway since nightfall.'

'Howcome you didn't see me getting back?'

'That's where you're wrong, mister. I did see you getting back. I saw you come up in your car. I saw every move you made. Look, if you're going to operate a one-man dragnet I could come along and help.'

I stared at the guy for several seconds. He had put his gun out of sight and I played with the idea of pulling my own gun on him and searching him for a pocket transmitter. I let the idea ride. Somehow I couldn't see Sam as Sandra's tormentor. And didn't I know who her tormenter was, any-way—that mug who had beefed me in the beach-hut at White Surf Bay. Sure. But there were strings running from the mug that somebody else was holding on to. He was nothing better than a puppet, jumping when he was told to jump. It was the manipulator I wanted a quiet word with.

'All right,' I said. 'If you want to make yourself useful, spread yourself over the east side of the grounds. I'll take the west side.'

'What are we looking for—some kind of damn ghost?'

'Could be. Tell me, you haven't heard traffic going past within the last hour? Could you hear traffic on the road from this far back?'

'Yeah, you can. I heard quite a few cars. None of them came along the driveway.'

'Get to it, Sam. And mind what you're doing with that gun. I don't want to wind up dead before I sort this case out for Sandra.'

'Wouldn't I laugh to bust a gut,' Sam sniggered and headed off into the shadows.

Alone, I regretted recruiting the mutt's aid. He might be a trigger-happy character, just waiting for the opportunity to drop a slug in somebody like me.

I worked over towards the patio, then scouted the perimeter of the swimming pool. From there I took in the lawns, edging gradually to the fringe of trees that flanked the grounds on the west side.

Five minutes later I stopped and brought a cigarette to my lips. Something told me not to light it. I didn't know what. A sixth sense. A prescience. It was uncanny. I flipped the cigarette away from me. I wondered howcome I was suddenly psychic.

There was a brisk breeze blowing down off the hills and it sang and blustered through the higher branches. My hand went to my waistband and came away holding the .38. Instinctively I pushed off the safety.

Before me was nothing but the smooth lawns, reflecting the overhead pattern of clouds and moonglow. I narrowed my eyes to pick out the thick stuff growing over yonder on the east side. I thought I saw the burly figure of Sam Walton, but I couldn't be sure.

Suddenly there was a hoarse curse. It was followed by some-one thrashing in the undergrowth. Then a yell.

'Muller, I see him. I see him!'

I was sprinting towards the shout when the shot came. It was a single, staccato explosion. A man cried out, groaned.

'Muller, Muller...'

He was down on the ground when I reached him, lying on his back and panting like his lungs couldn't grab enough air. It was Sam Walton for sure, and I bent over him.

'Are you hit, Sam?'

He tried to answer me, but couldn't. It was a damnfool question in any case. Sam had been hit all right, and then some. Dark stain was taking possession of his shirtfront, spreading in an ugly ragged blob.

I jerked up when I heard the dim hammer of running feet. The feet were racing, not towards the rear of the big house, but off to the west, intent on gaining the scrubland beyond the Hillview boundary.

'I'm going after him, Sam.'

'Yeah... You do that, Muller...'

The voice was nothing but a bubbling whisper and fading fast. I loped off and left him. I crashed into a dense thicket and was flung forward on my hands and face. I scrambled up and kept running, and a long time later I had lost the gunman and lost my sense of direction into the bargain.

The hills crouched around me in the feeble moonlight. I was on some kind of dirt track that snaked into a hollow and out of it again. A car engine surged to life. It wasn't more than a dozen yards away, and the reason I hadn't seen it was on account of it having been hidden in a cluster of huge boulders.

When its headlamps came on they trapped me in their

concentrated flare the way a moth is trapped by a light bulb.

'Run, you stupid punk,' a voice shrieked in my mind. 'If you don't he's going to mangle you into pulp.'

The car screamed and writhed across the uneven ground. I spurted for the side of the track and the damn thing ploughed after me like it couldn't resist me. I made a wild jump that would have made an Olympic champion blush with envy, hit my ankle on a rock and did a somersault into a ditch.

There was a shriek of tyres, a grind of brakes. I glimpsed the car leaving the ground in a brilliant take-off, speed through the air and slam down mightily on its suspension. It went on like a bat out of hades, and two minutes later had vanished from sight over the lip of the hollow.

I squatted for a while and smoked a cigarette. Then I remembered Sam Walton and set about finding my way back to him. It seemed that a month must have passed before I reached the spot where I'd left the poor sap. He was still there, but by now he was stone dead.

I realized I wasn't alone anymore. People were spreading over the lawns. I recognized Dirk Williams giving curt orders.

'Don't do anything silly,' the actor was saying. 'Sam isn't at the front of the house. Muller is missing. It's hard to say what the hell's going on around here. I never trusted that guy Muller from the start.'

'You're just prejudiced,' Gale Bush said in my defence. 'Look out, Hackett, you're tramping all over me.'

'Sorry, Miss Bush. It's so hard to see.'

'You can say that again,' Rachel Collins spat savagely. 'And my money is on Mr Williams. That Muller has a mean mouth and a lewd eye. He'd rape a cat if it stood still for long enough.'

'Oh, for heaven's sake, Rachel,' Gale snapped. 'Mr Muller hasn't raped anybody.'

'You seem pretty sure of it,' Dirk Williams said sarcastically. 'You pretend to know more about Muller than the rest of us.'

'You shut your big mouth, Dirk,' the petite blonde snarled. 'If you don't you're going to find a shoe mixed up in your back teeth. Look, there's nobody here. Let's get back to Sandra.'

'Let's call the cops,' Rachel said. 'I had a bad feeling. I smelt it. It was everywhere in the air. The smell of death.'

'No cops,' Williams gritted. 'Likely they've both taken cold feet and cleared off. Good riddance, I say.'

At that point I showed myself and called to Williams.

'Over here, Dirk. The rest of you stay where you are.'

They all fell silent. They all froze in their tracks. It was Gale who took the initiative and began walking towards me.

'What is it, Paul?' she cried anxiously. 'We thought we heard a shot. Paul!' she shrieked. 'You're not—'

'I'm okay,' I said. 'But Sam isn't.'

Gale didn't come any further. Williams did. He walked across the lawn slowly, then halted when he made out the form of Sam Walton at my feet.

'He's killed him!' he moaned. 'He's murdered Sam.'

'Pull yourself together, punk. I didn't kill Sam. Somebody did kill him, though.'

'You're a liar, Muller. A dirty liar! We heard the shot. It was your gun we heard. You can't deny it. You killed him. Now we're ruined,' he panted. 'Ruined! Oh, you horrible, mean-tempered bastard...'

He was asking for it and he got it. I clipped him on the point of the chin. Not too hard, but hard enough to put him sprawling on the broad of his back.

By this time Collins was shrieking to start a riot. Hackett gripped her and shook her and told her to calm down. She shrieked all the louder and took off back to the house.

'Why did you do it, Paul?' Gale cried in a strangled voice.

'But hell, I didn't do it, baby.'

'Don't baby her, you big bastard,' Williams raved. He heaved himself to his feet and backed off to join Gale. Then they began backing off together.

'The police,' Gale choked. 'We'll have to get the police!'

It was ten minutes afterwards when they arrived.

CHAPTER TWELVE

In no time at all they threw a cordon around Hillview. Search-lights were set up to enable measurements to be taken. The medical examiner did his stuff on Sam and pronounced him dead beyond all doubt. The lab boys went to work. The body of Sam Walton was taken away in a meat wagon. It was all too much for Jude Tripp.

He had been Sam's pal, he said. They'd grown up together, practically, went to school together, high school; they never did make it to college, which wasn't surprising, I figured, when everything was taken into consideration.

Now Sam Walton was dead and Jude didn't have one tiny doubt in his brain about who had killed him. Muller had killed him.

'You'd better watch your step,' Sergeant Garson advised Tripp. Garson was the homicide man in charge of the operation. On arrival he had demanded an inventory of the residents of Hillview, permanent and temporary. Then he had herded all of us into the big drawing-room. Oddly enough, although Garson had agreed to Dirk Williams' request that Sandra be permitted to remain in her bedroom, Sandra had insisted on being present with the rest of us.

Now the lab gang and technicians had departed. Garson had sent a detail of men to scour the grounds and outlying scrub country. Garson had listened to my story but hadn't bothered to hide his belief that I might be a damn liar.

He was a tall, blocky man, with bleak eyes and a cynical

mouth, and he stood there in the centre of the floor while we sat around him like a lot of guilty juveniles and waited for him to decide what punishment he ought to dish out.

'I'm inclined to back up Jude,' Dirk Williams declared stubbornly in defiance of the Sergeant's advice. His dark eyes glittered malevolently on me as he spoke. 'What Muller says about a man shooting Sam and then skipping for a car hidden in the rocks is nothing less than a cock-and-bull story.'

'Oh, yeah?' I said frigidly. 'So I told a cock-and-bull story, did I? Then how do you think my clothes got in such a state? Where did I get these scrapes and scratches? And just take a look at my ankle, Dirk baby. I'll be a lucky guy if I can walk on it inside the next twelve months.'

'You'll be lucky if you need to walk on it inside the next twelve months,' the punk sneered.

'Now see here, Mr goddamn Loudmouth—

'Shut up, Muller,' Garson snapped sharply. 'You too, Williams.'

'*Mr* Williams, if you please, Sergeant.'

'Yeah. Okay. But button your lip, buster, and speak when you're spoken to. I want to get this thing straight. I know it's too much to expect a calm and reasonable explanation from any of you—'

'Oh, but you're wrong, Sergeant,' Gale Bush broke in sweetly.

Garson had a hard gander at the blonde from the feet right along to her face. His gaze stopped at two places on the trip and then a weak smile wrapped his mouth. He consulted a notepad he held in one hand.

'You're Sandra Marsh.'

'I am Sandra Marsh,' Sandra contributed in a small voice.

'Sorry, Miss Marsh. So you are. How could anybody be mistaken? I watched your last series. I never missed a show. It was a positive success.'

He gave Sandra the same treatment he had given Gale. This time it took him quite a while to get over the obvious hurdles.

'You were saying, Sarge,' I nudged him.

He cleared his throat and threw me an icy scowl. He looked at his notepad. 'Yeah. Well okay. Lets get it straight. You're Miss Gale Bush, right?'

'Right,' Gale smiled. 'And—'

'Just a second, Miss Bush. For the record, let's get the list straight.'

I sighed heavily and fingered a cigarette to my lips. Garson flung me another scowl before continuing.

'You,' he said to the houseboy, 'are Frank Hackett.'

'That's right, Captain, and if you want—'

'I don't want anything from you at the moment, pal. Try and make this as easy for everyone as is possible.' He shifted his attention to the maid and went on another long journey. 'You are Petra Holbrooke.' Petra nodded dumbly and drew her nightdress across her knees defensively. 'And you,' he said to Rachel Collins, 'are Rachel Collins.'

'Of course I'm Rachel Collins,' the biddy said curtly. 'But I never saw this happening at the movies.'

Garson coloured and said, 'Huh? What has the movies got to do with it, ma'am?'

'Oh, never mind,' Collins sniffed. 'All I know it's a queer way to catch a killer.'

'We'll catch the killer,' Garson retorted stiffly. 'Don't you worry. Now you,' he addressed Jude Tripp, 'are Jude Tripp.'

'I figured I was,' Jude replied morosely. 'I figured Sam and me were doing ourselves a good turn when Mr Williams asked us to act as Miss Marsh's bodyguard. Nobody said we were going to get murdered.'

'Naturally,' Dirk Williams spat feelingly. 'But then Muller

here arrived on the scene, and—'

'For the last time, buster,' Garson interrupted him, 'shut up and speak only when you're spoken to. Now,' he continued patiently, 'the picture that I have is this: eariler on Miss Marsh suffered some sort of nightmare. It brought the whole house awake. One of her bodyguards—Tripp—was stationed inside the house, and the other was stationed outside. You placed the bodyguards, Mr Williams?'

'So what?' Dirk snorted defiantly. 'It was my job, wasn't it? Sure, I placed them. But what reason had Muller to go out of the house?'

It was a question that Garson expected me to answer. When I went on calmly puffing at my cigarette he began to colour up again.

'Why did you go out of the house, Muller?'

'I couldn't get to sleep again after being roused. I felt cramped, kind of. I needed fresh air. So I went for a walk.'

'Then you met up with Sam Walton and the two of you decided it would be a ball to go walking together?'

'Like I said at the beginning, chief, we heard a noise in the grounds. We separated to investigate. Sam took one side of the grounds and I took the other.'

'Then you shot him,' Dirk Williams cried. 'Why don't you go ahead and admit it, Muller, and save everybody a lot of time and trouble?'

I got out of my chair to cross to Dirk and Garson grabbed my shoulder and slammed me back into the chair. He was seething like a boiler about to burst. He brought a gun from his pocket. I recognized it as the gun he had taken when he'd frisked me. He held it extended in the palm of his hand.

'This is Muller's gun. It's a .38 Smith and Wesson. It hasn't been fired recently. According to the medical examiner's preliminary findings, Sam Walton was knocked out by a big slug more like a .45. According to the medical examiner also, the slug is lodged in the body. It will be checked when removed. Then we'll try and find the gun that fired it.'

'You know, Sarge,' I said admiringly, 'you make it all sound so lucid and simple. And isn't it a wonder that pal Dirk still fails to grasp the point.'

'You could have had two guns,' Williams raged. 'You used one of them to shoot Sam and kept the other for an alibi.'

'Sure. And what did I do with the .45—make a meal of it before the cops got here? Grow up, old buddy. I might have thrown it away, but if I did the cops will find it.'

Garson wound up his session shortly after this. Nobody was to go anywhere beyond the limits of Burville until they had permission to do so.

'I'm leaving an officer on guard duty for the remainder of the night, Miss Marsh,' he said to Sandra. 'You, Muller, I want to see at my office at headquarters before noon tomorrow.'

'Anything to oblige, chief. And mind the bottom step on your way out. It's kind of slippery and you might fall down and do something to your head.'

He gave me the full works with his bleak, laser-beam eyes, said a gruff goodbye to Sandra, and headed for the front door, accompanied by Hackett.

When he'd gone an atmosphere of unrelieved gloom took possession of the drawing-room. Collins excused herself and went off to bed.

'I'll need at least half an hour's sleep before I start in to get breakfast ready,' she shot back from the doorway.

Next Sandra told Petra and Hackett they were excused. It left the five of us there—Sandra, Gale, Dirk, Jude and myself —and before Williams could renew his campaign against me I rose and headed for the drawing-room exit.

'Where are you off to, Muller?' Dirk demanded bitingly.

'To bed, Dirk. Like Collins said, we need some sleep ere the dawn.'

'It's a wonder your conscience will allow you to sleep,' the guy yammered. 'I know if—'

'Let me tell you something you don't know, sugar,' I interrupted him. 'Give me one more word of that "You killed Sam" crap and, so help me, I'll break every bone in your miserable, insignificant body.'

Williams lunged out of his chair, waving his arms frantically. 'Sandra, if you don't get rid of this louse immediately I'll—I'll—'

'What will you do, Dirk?' Gale asked curiously when he suddenly became tongue-tied.

'I'll walk out of this affair at once,' he declared threateningly. 'So you'd better make up your mind, Sandra.'

I stood there by the door and waited to see what the actress's reaction would be. Her gaze shuttled between me and Williams for a moment, then she inclined her head slowly as though in acceptance of his ultimatum.

'I have hired Mr Muller, Dirk. He is going to remain hired until he has earned the money I am paying him.'

I thought the guy might topple down in a faint with the shock. He withstood it manfully, running his manicured fingers across his head nervously. His anger fanned itself to a real fury.

'Then you doubt my judgment, Sandra? My advice is meaningless to you. I—'

'Knock it off,' I cut in on him. 'Why don't you take the Sergeant's tip and give everybody a break, Dirk? Shut your goddamn mouth before something gets in there and cripples the machinery—for good,' I ended on a bleak note and went on out of the room, slamming the door behind me.

I hadn't gone more than a dozen steps towards the staircase

until somebody rushed after me and called my name.

'Mr Muller—Paul—wait!'

'Wait for what?' I said to Sandra. 'Another minute in that guy's company and I'd puke. You might have taste, baby, but it's rank bad taste when it comes to picking would-be husbands. Give me little old Al Hoseck on any day of the week—nude paintings and all. At least he gets the message when he's beaten.'

'Paul!' she chided. 'I'm disappointed in you. Really I am. But Dirk apart, I want to talk with you. Where—where are you going?'

'I'm going to my bedroom,' I told her. 'It's about the last refuge I've got in this house.'

'Then I can come with you? To talk,' she added blushingly when my eyes lit up at the idea.

'You ought to know what you're doing, Sandra. Say, maybe we should tote a bottle up with us...'

'No bottle,' she said frostily.

'Suit yourself, honey,' I shrugged. 'After you. But if you think this trick will do anything constructive towards endearing Dirk to me, then you're pretty wide of the mark.'

We went into my bedroom and I closed the door behind us. I offered Sandra a cigarette and lit one for myself. I sat down on the edge of the bed and took a chair that was close to the door.

'Now, Paul,' she began in a business-like tone, 'don't you feel that we ought to tell the police the truth. The whole truth. About the radio receiver you found. Your real reason for going out of the house tonight. You went out to try and find whoever was in possession of the transmitter, did you not?'

'Yeah, I did,' I admitted. I yawned. My ankle hurt like ninety.

'Then—then the rest happened exactly as you told Sergeant

Garson it did?'

'More or less. I told Sam I was going to have a look over the grounds. He volunteered to help and I let him. I told him to search the east side and I would take the west side. A little while later he called to me. He said he had seen someone. Then there was a shot. Sam was dying when I reached him—'

'Yet you left him and went on in order to overtake the gunman?'

'That's right, Sandra. You might say it was a callous act, and maybe it was. But Sam would have died anyhow. I lost my way, wound up out yonder in the open country. Next thing a car was being driven at me. I jumped for it—proving that my ballet lessons weren't a complete waste of time—received a few scratches and bruises, made it back to Sam, and here I am.'

She studied me in silence for the space of a whole minute.

'It was terrible,' she said finally and shuddered. 'And you're a very brave man, Paul.'

'Of course I'm a very brave man. Have I not decided to spend the rest of the night under this roof. With a guy like Dirk Williams trying to hog the whole stage! That takes some doing.'

She tried to smile. It was a valiant effort, but it didn't quite make the grade. She really was an eyeful, and, had the overall mood been a trifle more upbeat, I might have given her a demonstration of sheer courage. As it was, we sat there and studied each other, like overgrown versions of Jack and Jill.

'I think we ought to tell Sergeant Garson the truth, Paul,' she said again. 'There's no doubt that the radio receiver is a direct link with the killer of Sam. It would hardly be fair to withhold any of the facts. The police are deserving of all the clues that are available.'

I shrugged and got another cigarette going.

'You're the boss, Sandra. If you want to tell Garson, then you must go ahead and tell him. I don't think you should. This killer will run for cover. He might stay under cover from here on out, or he might not. The radio receiver is a clue he doesn't know we've got. Bring it into the open and you weaken the chances of trapping him.'

'You—you would advise me to keep quiet, then?'

'I'd advise you to say no more than it is absolutely necessary to say, honey. You could have had the police at the beginning had you wanted them. You figured your reputation might suffer as a result. I don't know whether or not it would. But you've ridden this far solo and there isn't much percentage in filling up the boat with cops.'

She asked me for another cigarette and I gave her one. Now her gaze was searching on me, like she had something special on her mind.

'I've got this feeling, Paul,' she said thoughtfully. 'I would like to know if it carries any weight. Do you know any more than you've told me to date?'

'I've got a couple of sour hunches,' I said. 'A few feeble guesses. At this stage they're only half-hatched.'

'I see,' she said dubiously. 'Let's put it another way. Do you have any real hopes of getting to the bottom of the mystery?'

'Let's put it my way,' I told her with a grin. 'On the instant I feel like calling Uncle, I'll tell you immediately.'

It wasn't quite what she hoped for, but it was all I could give her right then. She rose from the chair, came across to the bedside table to mash her cigarette into an ashtray. She stood for a moment and gazed steadily into my face.

'You won't let me down, Paul.'

'I won't let you down, baby.'

She leaned over and laid a cool kiss on my lips, then left me and headed for the door. She halted there and glanced back across her shoulder.

'How do you find Gale, Paul?'

'Real keen,' I said. 'Why?'

'Don't overstep the boundaries,' she told me. 'Gale is my very good friend. I wouldn't want anything to happen to her.'

I said nothing and she went on out.

I didn't get into bed directly. I stripped off and had a look at the bruises I'd taken. They weren't so bad. I thought about Sam Walton and decided that was real bad.

I rolled into bed finally. I dreamed. Dirk Williams had found the concealed radio receiver and was using it as a microphone.

'I'm telling you, folks, it was Muller who murdered Sam. Sam was my bosom buddy. We went to school together. We grew up together. He shot Sam in the back. Now I can't marry Sandra.'

It was crazy and not at all like my usual dreams. I usually dream about dames. I was glad when I awoke and discovered it was bright morning time. I got up, showered, shaved, and went down to have breakfast.

When I reached the dining-room Gale was the only person at the table. She gave me a big smile and a feeble hello. Everybody else was pounding pillows, she said. Life was a drag, wasn't it? Well, her idea of passing the time was kicking her heels in the air, having fun. And what was so commendable about carrying a hundred-pound sack of woe around on your shoulders, she added reasonably.

'You don't have to grin and bear it,' I told her and took a chair opposite her. The food was on a trolley and we had to help ourselves. 'I mean, if your wagon bogs down, you can always hitch it to another star. And it doesn't necessarily have to be called Sandra Marsh.'

'You expect me to run off and leave her in the lurch, Paul? But I wouldn't behave so to a sick dog.'

'I don't expect you to do anything, baby,' I said and added cream to my coffee.

'But I can do it real good when I get around to it, huh?' she giggled.

'Yeah,' I said with sincerity. 'You sure can, lollipop. I—'

At that instant the door opened and Petra put her head through. 'I'm sorry to disturb you, Mr Muller, but Miss Marsh would like to see you immediately.'

'Oh, no!' Gale groaned. 'Don't tell me it has happened again.'

It wasn't another telephone call that was worrying Sandra, I discovered a few minutes later when I joined the TV star in her bedroom.

'It's gone, Paul,' she said in a shocked voice, pointing at the window ledge. 'I had a look just now when I awoke. Don't you see what it means,' she went on shakily. 'Someone must have taken advantage of all the fuss earlier to make off with the receiver...'

CHAPTER THIRTEEN

I dropped in at police headquarters around eleven o'clock. I didn't see Garson at once, but was shown into a room and asked to dictate a formal statement concerning my involvement in last night's killing. I made the statement—which hardly varied more than a few words from what I'd already said to Garson—signed it, and was told to wait until the sergeant was free.

'So long as he doesn't make a suspense story out of it. I'm a busy beaver and I like to keep weaving.'

'Yeah?' the officer who was leaving me said. He was a young guy, still damp behind the ears, and he stared at me like I was some new species from outer space. 'You're a private detective, Mr Muller. Gee, why didn't I think of it before becoming a policeman!'

Garson sent through for me five minutes later. He was crouching behind a scarred desk like a bullfrog who had been defending the same lily-pad for years and wasn't going to give it up just because it was out of style. He had shaved, and yet his square chin retained a marring darkness, as if his face carried its own shadow around with it, just to scare the hell out of fresh-skinned rookies like the one who'd entertained me earlier.

'Take a seat, Mr Muller,' he said tolerantly and gestured to the only other chair in the cubby-hole. 'Cigarette?'

'Thanks,' I said and got up again to accept a battered cylinder from a crumpled pack.

'Now,' he said briskly when we were both smoking, and stabbed a blunt finger at the statement before him. 'Your report kind of surprises me, Mr Muller.'

'It does? I didn't intend it to, Sarge. I gave the bald facts in the only kind of English I know. You mean I should have gone into the gory details? How Sam panted his last breath. How he bled so much before he died—'

'I mean nothing of the sort,' Garson snarled. 'You gave the bald facts right enough—if they are the facts. The trouble is they're too bald for my liking. What do you tell us? You tell us practically nothing.'

'But, Sarge—'

'Cut out this Sarge stuff,' he said angrily. 'I've been on with Anfield, mister. I got your measure from the department over there. They tell me you're a wise guy. They tell me that when you're around, murder just naturally happens. They tell me all manner of intriguing things about your way with dames ...'

'Now hold it right there, chief,' I broke in on him. 'Who's talking about dames anyhow? What's the matter with you— are you sexually repressed, frustrated?'

'That's something else they tell me,' Garson thundered. 'You make a hobby of tweaking police officers' tails. Well—' He thumped the ailing desk with a massive fist. '—I've got one tail you're not going to tweak—

'You must be kidding, Sarge.'

'I'm not kidding, Muller. I'm serious. I've got enough here to slam you into a cell. How would you like that, huh? I could keep you here for a day, a week; indefinitely, even!'

I let him blow off his steam for all he was worth. It was nothing more than a variation of the chest-thumping routine that all cops with miniature brains and big egos feel they must demonstrate for my benefit. When he had simmered down I dropped his cigarette to the floor and put my heel on it. Then I brought out a Lucky and took my time over lighting it. Garson's jaws went a dull brick colour and he breathed heavily down his nose.

'Are you quite finished, Sarge?' I asked calmly. 'Because if you are I've got better things to do than sit here and listen to a load of juvenile abuse. You've got my statement there. It says what I know about the Sam Walton killing and it says nothing but the truth.'

'I'm not finished, Muller. Not by a long chalk. You're not out at the Sandra Marsh mansion for the good of your health, I bet. Okay, you've got a thing for plain and simple language. So use it to tell me why this dame has hired you.'

'Sorry, Sarge,' I told him after a short pause, 'I never discuss my clients or their reasons for hiring me.'

'You admit she did hire you? Why?'

'I've just explained—'

'Yeah, you have,' he snorted with a thick sneer. 'You don't talk about your clients. Well, it so happens that someone at Hillview has displayed a sense of responsibility to the society he lives in and depends upon for protection.'

He paused there himself to let it sink in. It did sink in—right under my belt. Was the guy merely pulling a tall bluff in the hope that I'd walk into his trap, or had somebody at Hillview really blown the gaff on Sandra's misery?

Garson's mean lips curled mockingly.

'You think I'm whistling in the dark, shamus? Okay. Then listen. Sandra Marsh has been having threatening messages in the form of phone calls. It was the reason that Dirk Williams character brought on Jude Tripp and Sam Walton to perform as muscle-men. Williams figured they were all the protection the dame needed. Then she heard of you. She went to Anfield and put up at a hotel. The Rialto, if you want me to prove

I know what I'm talking about. She asked you to move in at Hillview and to set about solving her problem.

'I don't know what progress you've made. If you've made any progress I want to hear what it is. The phone calls might have seemed to be nothing worse than the ravings of a nut until last night. Last night changed everything. A man was loose in the grounds at Hillview. He was challenged by Walton and shot Walton deader than a dodo. That means he's a killer. My job is to catch killers before they get a taste for blood and go on to make a habit of killing. You'll agree it makes sense?'

'But you haven't caught this killer?'

'Of course I haven't caught him. But don't worry, I will. In the meantime, do we or do we not have your co-operation, pal?'

'You think I'll make it tough for you, Sarge, just so it might provide the opportunity to strip me of my licence? Well, I won't make it tough for you. I'm a big-hearted guy. I don't go for killers, myself.'

'Then I can bank on you?' Garson asked eagerly. 'Right up to the hilt?'

'Further than the hilt,' I said generously.

'Hell, Muller,' he said sheepishly, 'maybe you're not such a bad joe after all.'

'I'm glad you look at it that way, Sarge,' I said warmly.

'Swell, just swell! Well, we mustn't waste any time, Paul, so how about getting on with it.'

I said, 'Huh?'

Garson began to colour again slowly. He took a deep breath and held it for ten seconds—just like his psychiatrist had advised him, probably—then he let it whistle gently through his lips. He smiled weakly and it must have subjected his facial muscles to exquisite torture.

'Tell me what you know, Muller,' he murmured tautly. 'Everything. Down to the last bald detail.'

'I hate to disappoint you, chief,' I told him regretfully. 'But you really shouldn't lay all of your money on a single horse.'

Garson slammed the desk again and stormed to his feet.

'All right, you screwed-up punk,' he roared. 'If that's the way you want to play it, then okay. But remember, mister, give me one good reason for hauling you in, and so help me, you goddamn gumshoe, I'll have you behind bars quicker than you can think.'

I went over to the door and opened it. Garson was close to having a fit when I halted and looked back at him.

'Well,' he grated. 'What are you waiting for?'

'Just for the dust to settle down, chief. It tends to cling, kind of, and why taint the air outside that folks have to breathe?'

Garson was erupting all over the place when I left him. I got into the Jag and drove to a phone booth. I shut myself inside and dialled the Hillview number. It was Gale who came on and I told her I wanted to speak to her alter-ego.

'Lay off that brand of talk, Paul,' she chided me coldly. 'If you ever had any doubts regarding my gender they're surely laid to rest by this time.'

'Of course they are, baby. And I never doubted you for a moment. But put me on with the leading lady in the drama like a good little gal.'

'You've dug up something?' Gale asked curiously.

'Nothing to write a song about. Buzz, honey-bee.'

I had Sandra's attention a half minute later.

'Yes, Paul?' she said anxiously. 'What is it?'

'I've been to police headquarters to pay my respects, Sandra. This guy Garson—the homicide dick—it seems he's managed to rig up a hotline with Hillview. In other words, baby, he's in possession of a handful of home truths. He knows why Dirk hired Jude and Sam, and why you decided to hire me.'

'He does! Oh, but this is awful, Paul. Who—who would have told him?'

'Don't ask me, Sandra. You're sure you didn't make a clean breast, hoping he would treat the news in confidence?'

'No, no, I didn't. I'm surprised at you thinking such a thing. You're saying that someone here revealed everything behind my back?'

'Practically everything, honey. So you don't have to be an expert in mathematics to do this kind of poser. Problem one, who placed the radio receiver on your window ledge? Two, who took it away again? Three—are you getting me loud and clear, Sandra?'

'Yes, Paul, I am,' she said in a faltering voice. 'I know what the third problem is. Who contacted the police and gave them the information?'

'Nice going,' I complimented her. 'Then put your mental processes to work,' I went on. 'I've been doing it and I've got one very nasty answer so far.'

'Someone here is really mixed up in it?' she groaned. 'Oh, you hinted so before, Paul, but I wouldn't listen to you. Yes, you must be right. But no, you're not!' she almost shrieked. 'Everyone here at Hillview is my friend. I refuse to believe I am being subjected to this hellish torture from anyone inside the house.'

'If that's how you feel, then you must suit yourself, Sandra.'

'You sound disappointed in me,' she rejoined weakly.

'Let's say I'm sorry for you,' I told her. 'I'm sorry for anybody who refuses to face up to life.'

'All right, damn it, Paul! You don't have to rub it in. I'll go along with anything you say. You're saying that someone here hates me badly enough to do me harm. But who is it?

Dirk? Gale? One of the staff?'

'Slow down. I don't know. I'm keeping an open mind.'

'Would you claim that this person is the one who got in touch with the police since the killing of Sam Walton?'

'No, I wouldn't,' I replied after a short pause. 'Well, it would serve as a leading clue against him if it was. I'm inclined to the notion that whoever did tell the police has your interests at heart.'

'The sergeant might tell you if you asked him, Paul.'

'Not this sergeant, Sandra. I'm going to have to find out the hard way. In the meantime try and look on the bright side,' I added cheerfully.

'Bright side, he says! There just isn't a bright side to anything any more. I wish I had never got the part in the series, Paul. At least I wouldn't have to duck every time I hear a sound behind me. And, Paul...'

'Yeah?' I encouraged.

'The radio might have explained those voices and that terrible laughter I heard. But what about the man who somehow got into my bedroom? He couldn't have used a film projector? It sounds silly, I guess, but it occurred to me a little while ago.'

'Maybe it isn't so silly. Is Jude still sticking close by you?'

'Yes, he is. But somehow I don't think he has the same enthusiasm he evinced earlier.'

'I've got to go now, baby. See you soon.'

'Don't stay away for too long, Paul.'

I hung up and left the phone booth. I stood there in the street and watched the people go past, the traffic throb by like a mass of mechanized beetles. I got into the Jag and became one of the beetles, driving to Jefferson Avenue and wondering if there was anything to the jazz about the third time being lucky.

It turned out it was if I was willing to accept certain qualif-
ications. Julia Dortmeyer was at home when I knuckle-rapped
her door. The door opened and a blear-eyed brunette, who was
well-stacked and then some, stood peering at me. The dame
was three-quarters stoned, but had been drinking, I figured,
not for sheer joy of living, but to forget a lot of things that
had been happening to her up to this minute.

'Yeah?' she said recklessly, giving me a generous sample
of the reek on her breath. 'What do you want? If you're the
guy from the finance company then you can go jump a wall.
And don't ask me where the car is, because I don't have an
idea and I don't give a fiddler's curse.'

'That makes the both of us,' I said and gave her a big
smile.

'Hey!' she cried a moment later. 'How did you get in here?
I don't remember asking you in.'

'You don't?' I said and kicked the door shut with my heel.
'My, but you're developing a bad memory, Julia. You told me
to come in out of the cold.'

'I did—huh?' She passed a hand over her brow. She was
wearing a simple blue dress that had white spots on it, no
stockings, and suede mules on her tiny feet. She reminded me
of a rose that had blossomed about the time no one was watching, and now the blossom was full-blown and would be gone
come the next couple of winters. 'There's something knocking
around in my head,' she added vaguely. 'That old gasbag
under the stairs gave me a message— Yeah, now I've got it.
He said a man had been here, asking for me. Are you that
man, mister?'

'Could be I am, honey.' I went to a table and lifted the
bottle of forgetfulness she had been tippling from. There was
a paper cup and I poured a jolt and handed it to her. She

swiped the cup angrily to the floor and slumped down on a chair.

'Okay, buster,' she said resignedly. 'I knew something was bound to overtake me one of these days. You're a peeper, ain't you? No, don't bother to tell me about it. I know it all, mister, and then plenty after that. Which of those lushes are you representing—the wife of the supermarket executive or that load of whimsy that masquerades as Barney's wife? But don't tell me anyway! It doesn't matter a curse. Both of those guys would give an arm to get a divorce.'

'Julia,' I said carefully when I could get a word in. 'I'm not representing any lush. I'm just here to ask you a couple of questions about a certain actress that stole your limelight out at the Sunrise Studios...'

'Sandra Marsh!' she panted and grabbed for the bottle on the table. 'What do you know about that two-timing daughter of a bitch? What do you know about me, come to that?'

'Slow down, beautiful,' I told her and removed the bottle from her fingers. I had a swig from the neck before placing it well out of her reach. 'I don't know much about Sandra. I know even less about you—'

'That so?' she cried belligerently. 'Well, I can tell you plenty about her. She's a bitch for a starter. She'd steal the pennies out of a blind man's tin. She'd—'

'So you don't actually love her, Julia?'

She stared at me for the space of twenty seconds. She tried to blink the haze from her eyes. The haze refused to go away and she made a swatting gesture with her hand.

'Okay, peeper,' she said. 'What's the use? I got a raw deal and I'm not going to fill a basin with tears. It was the luck of the draw, maybe. That and the big yen Mr goddamn Goldman had to get her into the sack. So what do you want to hear about—how I hate her guts?'

'Goldman was fond of her, Julia?'

'Didn't I just tell you. It made George unique at the studios. Everybody else there detested the dirty— But say, what is all this about anyhow? Nothing has happened to Sandra? Well, I wouldn't want to hear anything more than she had been run over by a truck or had a knife stuck in her back— But she's in trouble, isn't she?' the dame went on eagerly.

'You haven't been in touch with her recently, Julia?'

'Me! Have you lost your marbles? I wouldn't touch her with a ten-foot pole. Say, you're not accusing me of slitting her throat? Or maybe she was just shot and died cleanly?'

I gave her a cigarette and placed one in my own mouth. I studied her for a few moments. I came to the conclusion that calling on Julia was a mistake and a waste of time. I rose to go.

'You aren't in a hurry, big boy, are you?'

'Yeah, little girl. I am. Someone is annoying Sandra. Sending her nasty messages. You wouldn't know anything about that?'

'I wouldn't spend a stamp on her—even to send her a nasty message,' Julia said frankly.

'You wouldn't do it by phone? Or have somebody do it for you?'

'What do you take me for—a kook, a sadist? I've got my own row to hoe. Say, is she really living with that creep, Williams?'

'Not so you'd notice. He is a guest, though. As soon as he makes his name they're going to get married.'

'Excuse me while I sneeze! Dirk marry Sandra? Not when Gale Bush is around he won't.'

I'd been half-way through the doorway, but now I stalled and cocked my ears.

'You're slightly mixed-up, Julia, are you not? Sandra is Dirk's passion flower and not Gale.'

'Have it any way you want it, big boy. But I recall the time—and it isn't too long ago—when Dirk and Gale were making the sweetest kind of music together. You don't believe me? Nobody's asking you to. But I saw them with my own eyes. Necking in Gale's dressing-room. And not only necking.' The dame rolled her eyes at the ceiling. She ran a pink tongue over her red lips. 'Say, do you really have to run, handsome? I could tell you plenty more might interest you. Got another bottle in the kitchenette...'

'Keep it on ice, Julia,' I told her. 'And thanks a million, doll. Maybe I'll do something for you sometime.'

'Just maybe, buster. I might be going at a low price these days, but nobody's gonna call me cheap.'

She was stretching for the bottle when I left her and closed the door gently behind me.

CHAPTER FOURTEEN

Sandra Marsh was waiting for me when I got back to Hillview. She appeared to have pulled herself together, and there was a more determined look about her—as though she had finally been brought face-to-face with every variety of torment there was and realized there were just two moves left for her to make. She could either go on beyond the fringe and go mad, or she could walk away from the fringe and defy the devil to do his worst.

I read it all there, written on her beautiful features, and my heart gave a queer lurch like the two of us could form a wonderful understanding, given the right foundation. Sandra must have been able to read a little of what was going on in my own mind and brought a feeble smile to bear.

'I'm glad to see you again, Paul. I have been watching out for you. There was a phone call shortly after you left. The caller rang for the third time a few minutes ago.'

'Oh,' I murmured. 'He didn't give his name.'

'He asked me to tell you that Larry wants to speak with you.'

She stared when I bustled past her into the house. She said I could use the phone in the lounge, then, when I sat down at the instrument and lifted it I found her standing at the door, an expectant arch to her eyebrows.

'This is kind of private, honey. Is it okay with you?'

'Of course.'

She blushed and left the room. There was nothing to hinder her cutting in on an extension when I raised Larry, but I didn't think she would. I couldn't understand why everybody hated her so. Everybody?

It was Milly Wheeler I raised first of all, and when we'd dispensed with the usual frills and fripperies I asked her if Larry Stern was in evidence.

'We've been in touch with your number three times, lover-boy. Three times a dame answered. What's going on at that end?'

'Nothing but a little fun,' I cracked. 'Go fetch Larry, passion flower.'

He was speaking to me a moment later.

'I've got some information for you, Paul,' he said. 'Do you want to get a pad to write it down?'

'I've got a good memory, chum. Just give, like a good guy. You did a check on the car?'

'Yeah. It belongs to a party called Bill Gibson. He has an address here in Anfield. But before I go any further, Paul, I think you should prepare to make notes.'

'Maybe you're right. Give me a minute.'

I had a ballpen in my jacket pocket but I didn't have much to write on. I crossed the lounge and found an envelope with Sandra's address on it. I split it and went back to my chair, lifted the phone.

'Go ahead, good friend, I'm ready now.'

'Gibson lives in an apartment on West Nation Street—'

'Skid Row, huh?'

'You know your own back yard as well as I do,' Larry said impatiently. 'The number is 684.'

'Does he live alone?'

'He's got a brother,' Larry said. 'His name is Walt. They live together. At the moment neither of them is employed, so far as I can gather. However, they did a stint a short while ago at a nightclub here. Bill acted as waiter and Walt helped out behind the bar.'

'You know the name of the joint?'

'The Bluebell on Central Avenue—'

'The Bluebell?' It triggered off something in my head that eluded me for ten seconds until I trapped it. The Bluebell was the place where I'd picked up Alice Ogden. Coincidence? Maybe. Just maybe. And when I reflected properly, it was Alice who had done the picking up that night. I'd been there lots of times, but had never noticed her before. Neither had I noticed a waiter who resembled the guy with the oil-blob eyes. Of course waiters, like assistant barhops, come and go, and I never pay much attention to them anyway.

'Can I go on,' Larry was saying drily. 'Or do you want a break to reminisce about old times?'

'Forgive me, Larry pal. I was thinking. You couldn't be more specific about the duration of the brothers' stay at the club?'

'I didn't know you would want it in hours and minutes,' Larry griped. 'I gathered they were there for only a week at the very outside.'

'Anything else?'

'A little. They've got a sister. She has done just about everything that's worth doing. Waitress, hatcheck girl, cigarette girl. You can guess the sort of stuff. It appears she started off with the idea of becoming a thrush, but her voice must have broken or something, and she jacked it up.'

'No fooling,' I said tautly. 'What would her name be— I'll Try Anything Gibson?'

'No, Larry said. 'She began life as Alice Gibson, but later she changed it to Ogden. Maybe some agent figured it would look better in neons.'

I felt my mouth going dry. I felt I wanted to spit, but there wasn't nearly enough moisture around to form a spit. I gave a little groan instead.

'What's wrong, Paul. Have I done you any good?'

'You're a sweetheart, chum. Have you reached the end of the line?'

'Almost. The rest could be called a postscript, I guess. Before coming to Anfield the Gibson boys did some real work in Burville. They shifted scenery, or polished camera lenses at the Sunrise TV Studios there. I couldn't get the right way of it.'

'You've got enough to make me happy, pal. Thanks a bunch, Larry.'

'Hey, wait a minute, bigbrain,' Larry growled. 'We don't devote all our resources to charity anymore. You mentioned cash, remember?'

'Sure, I did, and I'm a man of my word. You'll have a cheque in the mail.'

'For how much?' the guy grated suspiciously. 'We're off peanuts.'

'Five hundred bucks sweeten you up, sourpuss?'

'Say, you are on the make, Muller. For that kind of dough I wouldn't mind doing something else for you.'

'I'll think up something real cute and contact you when I do, Larry. Goodbye for now.'

I hung up and lit a cigarette. I was still stitting there by the phone and puffing furiously when the door opened and Gale Bush looked in.

'Sandra, I—' She broke off and peered around the room. 'I understood Sandra was in here, Paul. But she isn't, is she?'

'Not unless she can make herself invisible, honey. But who wants Sandra when you're around?' I added evenly.

Her brows came down in twin straight lines and she took a step further into the room. She was wearing cream shorts with a halter to match, and they clashed excitingly with the beautiful overall tan she had acquired. She glanced across her shoulder before closing the door behind her. She walked over to the cigarette pack I had laid down and fitted a cigarette to her lips.

'Was that supposed to be a joke, Paul?' she asked seriously. 'Or are you hinting at something that's lurking about beneath the surface?'

'I merely passed a remark,' I said innocently.

'Yeah,' she said. 'I heard it.' She sat down on a chair opposite and shuddered.

'Do you feel cold?'

'I feel like I've got an ice-bucket in place of a spine,' she confessed frankly. 'I thought I could shrug off what happened here last night, but I can't.'

'Why can't you? Why are you worried? You surely don't imagine the killer will make a mistake when he returns to kill Sandra, and kill you instead?'

'Paul Muller,' she yelped in horror, 'that isn't in the least funny. Why, it—it's positively ghoulish.'

'You're so right, baby. But there *was* a killer and he *did* kill Sam.'

She nodded and had a deep drag from her cigarette. She let the smoke stream from her nose.

'You went to police headquarters? They couldn't really hold you, of course, despite what Dirk may have said.'

'Dirk doesn't like me,' I said sadly. 'I wonder why.'

She stared at me for a half-minute. Her mouth curved in a small sensual smile and her eyes sparkled momentarily.

'You don't know, Paul? You can't even guess? It's obvious to me why he doesn't like you. You're everything he is not. Tall and rugged and manly, and—'

'Hold it right there, doll,' I said with a hard chuckle. 'I've got some hats I paid a lot of dough for. You go on like you're doing and my head won't fit them. Still, whatever Dirk thinks of me, I wouldn't want him to be left out of everything. But he has got Sandra, I guess.'

A frown crossed her features and was gone. She nodded. She rose and said impulsively, 'I'm going to make a drink. Want me to make it two?'

'So long as Sandra doesn't mind.'

'Why should she? We're her friends. We're under as much strain as she is.'

She did have a point and I told her so. She came back with a couple of highballs and resumed her seat in front of me.

'How did you get along with the police?'

'Not too well, I'm afraid. That Garson has a thing against private eyes.'

'He doesn't have any clues about the killing, did he say?'

'He didn't say, honey. I don't think he would have told me, even if he had.'

'There were more police here earlier,' she said. 'They scoured the grounds from one end to the other. Anyway,' she went on thoughtfully, 'the man who shot Sam Walton might not be the same person who is making those threats to Sandra.'

'Oh,' I murmured. 'The angle hadn't occurred to me. What was he doing in the grounds if he didn't come to draw the curtains like he said he would?'

'Perhaps he was a prowler,' Gale announced. 'You know— somebody who was trying to commit burglary. How do the police view it, Paul?'

I didn't answer her at once. There were a lot of things buzzing in my brain. Still, if the dame didn't get the news from me, she would likely hear it from the cops themselves before very long.

'You mean are they puzzled over a possible motive?'

She nodded and said it was exactly what she meant.

'Somebody spilled the beans to them,' I told her.

'What!' she cried. 'You're saying that after all the trouble Sandra has taken to keep those phone calls secret, some cheap loudmouth went and told the police? But who— Paul, you didn't do it, did you?'

'Who, me? Of course I didn't.'

'Then Sandra told them herself! Oh, the silly—'

'You're wrong, you know, Gale. Sandra didn't tell them. I gave her the tidings by phone, and she was horrified. But why make a song and dance over it? Once the cops get their teeth into a murder case no secret is sacred.'

Gale sighed and drained the contents of her glass. 'I suppose you're right. Once you climb to the top of a cliff and set a rock rolling, it isn't so easy to make it stop rolling...'

She paused and I waited for her to continue. She didn't. She put her glass away. She mashed her cigarette in a bowl and helped herself to another one from my pack. Then she kissed me on the cheek.

'I'm going to have a swim,' she said with a sort of reckless note in her voice. 'Come and join me and we'll make like we're two deep-sea divers.'

'Diving for what?'

'Pearls?'

I thought about her when she went away. I thought plenty. I imitated Gale's sigh, took my glass to the bottle and ice and made myself a drink, a large one. I had knocked about half of it back when I had a feeling I wasn't alone. I turned to face the lounge doorway and saw I was right. Dirk Williams stood just inside the door, a worried scowl hovering on his face.

'Hi, Dirk,' I greeted him casually. 'Looking for someone?'

'Yes,' he said in an oddly restrained manner. 'I've been

looking for you, Mr Muller.'

'I was so hard to find?'

He let it ride. He had the air of a man who had been doing a lot of solid thinking. He reminded me of a kid who has just tied a firecracker to a dog's tail and then come to admit it in true Georgie Washington style. I would much rather have had the old Dirk. That one you could have busted in the puss without suffering a dent in your conscience.

'Okay, pal,' I urged when he continued to regard me silently and gloomily, 'what's the matter? Have you used up the last of your nasty cracks?'

He winced a little and brought a refrigerated smile to his face. 'I want to apologize, Mr Muller,' he said evenly. 'Of course it wasn't you who shot Sam.'

'No fooling?' I said blankly. 'Did you get your information direct from the real killer, or are you just making another of your wild guesses?'

'Oh, hell, Muller,' he burst out impatiently. 'What do you want me to do—lie down and let you kick me? I've said I'm sorry, haven't I?'

'Okay, okay, don't blow a fuse. So you're sorry. So you don't think I killed Sam. Where do we go from here?'

'You're making it devilishly difficult for me,' he snorted. 'I've been thinking. I've concluded that we shouldn't be wasting our time and energy in senseless antagonism. After all, there is a great amount at stake here. This killer has struck once, and we have no idea when he'll strike again. Sandra is the real target, obviously. Therefore we ought to be linked in a common purpose.'

'That's what I call finding a grain of sense, pal,' I applauded and polished off my drink. 'Howcome you managed it all by yourself?'

'Then we can bury the hatchet, Paul?' he said eagerly. 'We

can combine our forces, pool our knowledge and findings?'

'Why not?' I said when I had mulled it over for a few seconds. 'You tell me exactly what you know, or think you know, and I'll take it on from there.'

His face fell noticeably. He did something interesting with his teeth. He looked like a thwarted fox now.

'So you don't trust me?' he accused. 'You think I'm not equipped to help you in any way whatever?'

'I didn't say so, Dirk. Look, why don't you fix yourself a drink and we'll do our best to find a real friendly footing?'

'What have you found out?' he said sharply, reverting somewhat to character. 'I've got a right to know, Muller. I demand to know what is going on. I demand to be kept informed, step by step, with relation to your investigations. If you fail to co-operate,' he ploughed on ominously. 'I shall advise Sandra in the strongest possible terms to curtail your activities immediately.'

'You will, huh? Don't you ever tire of carrying the weight of all that power around? You'll advise Sandra to do such and such? I wouldn't put it past you, either. Only what happens if she tells you politely to go tie a knot in your tail?'

His cheeks reddened and his eyes popped furiously.

'You're making fun of me,' he yammered. 'You're laughing at me! You underestimate me, Muller, as you'll soon find out to your cost. All right, you cheap, conniving bastard. Just wait and see who has the last laugh!'

'Are you quite finished, Dirk?'

I took a couple of steps towards the guy and he backed hastily to the exit, one hand raised defensively.

'Don't you lay a finger on me,' he quavered. He bolted on that note, slamming the door behind him.

I went to the bottle to pour another drink, changed my mind and went on out of the lounge. I found Rachel Collins in the kitchen, scrubbing at her pots and pans. She gave me a frigid look and demanded to know what I wanted there.

'I gotta rule,' she said. 'It's one of the conditions I stay here under. I guess you've heard how an Englishman's home is his castle, Muller. Well, this here is my domain and nobody plans an invasion without getting my permission first of all.'

'I only want a drink of water, Rachel. And I'm not planning on any invasion. Say, what's with the nervous flap-doodle, anyway? Did a dirty old man frighten you when you were in your teens?'

'Nobody frightened me, buster, and don't you forget it. But what am I saying! I'm as scared as hell. It's a wonder the pants haven't been scared right off me.'

'Maybe they have been, honeybunch,' I told her. 'Maybe too that was your reason for getting on with the cops and telling them the whole goddamn facts.'

For a minute I figured she would drop down in a dead faint. But the biddy was cut out of buffalo hide and she glared right back at me when she came out of her double-take.

'Where did you drag up that idea?' she hustled. 'Have you gone and told Miss Marsh that I'm nothing but a slack-mouthed busybody?'

'I haven't said a thing, Rachel. But it's still early days, and I just might light a fire under you if you don't come clean with me.'

She hemmed and she hawed and she rattled and clattered her pans around for a while. Then she wiped her hands on a towel and asked me for a cigarette. I gave her a cigarette and helped her to get it going.

'Okay, big fella,' she said finally. 'You're dead right. But I don't regret what I did for a single moment. There's too much cloak and dagger stuff going on here for my liking. That poor girl is ready to take off at the drop of a hat. Dirk Williams wants everybody to keep quiet. You want everybody to keep quiet. Hell, if everybody keeps his mouth buttoned, when is there going to be an end to it all? The cops wondered why that guy was prowling around. Well, I told them why he was prowling around. I told them about the phone calls, the laughter, the spook that was haunting Miss Marsh's bedroom. So okay, I told them. So you just go straight ahead and do your worst. At least it gives me an excuse for getting out of this bughouse.'

'Slow down, Rachel. Nobody's going to spill your beans.'

'Huh? You mean you're going to keep it all to yourself?'

'Yeah, I am. So now we've got something in common, baby. You sing dumb and I'll sing dumb. And now, how about that drink of water? The liquor round here tastes like the stuff that's left when you wash the dishes.'

CHAPTER FIFTEEN

Jude Tripp was sitting beside the swimming pool, watching Gale Bush go through some pretty spectacular dives. At the far side of the pool Sandra Marsh reclined in the sunshine. She was wearing a cool, white linen dress and was smoking a cigarette. She was watching Gale as well, or so it seemed. She had dark sun-glasses on and I couldn't say for an absolute certainty what she was watching.

As I came off the patio she raised her head. She started to make a gesture, but then changed her mind and addressed her attention to the petite blonde. Even at this distance I could sense the air of tension surrounding Sandra. She had girded herself to meet the inevitable, if the inevitable must happen. It was the impression she gave me and I couldn't help wondering if it was a valid one. Was she as frightened as she appeared to be??

Gale Bush was quite a versatile dame, I figured, switching my gaze to her. She was climbing the rungs to the high board at that moment and her wet, tanned body reflected the brilliant sunlight in an excitingly sensual way. Her two-piece bikini just thumbed its nose at convention and let her lush curves have the maximum of freedom, which was what they wanted, anyway. Poised, she looked down and across the pool and saw me. She waved her hand. Tripp didn't know I was there and he gave a low chuckle and waved back.

I cleared my throat and he turned his head quickly, disappointment making his blunt features lugubrious.

'You just had to spoil it for me, Muller, didn't you,' he grunted. 'Why couldn't you—'

'You've still got your dreams, Jude,' I broke in comfortingly. 'And nobody can take them away from you,' I added profoundly.

'Oh, yeah! You think you're smart. You give me a pain, friend. Right where I'm sitting down. Say! Get a load of that dive,' he sidetracked enthusiastically as Gale's small body knifed the surface of the pool and vanished.

It seemed she was taking a long time to reappear and Jude was leaning forward concernedly when Gale bobbed up at the edge nearest us.

'Hi, fellas,' she greeted. 'Why don't you come on in and join the fun?'

She was watching me steadily as she spoke, but Jude immediately began pulling at his shirt. He whipped it free of his belt and bared his fat stomach.

'Hey, wait a minute,' I said to the guy. 'You're wearing swim-trunks beneath your pants, maybe?'

'Cheese!' he said. 'It's a good thing you stopped me, Muller. I musta got carried away.'

'You get into that pool without trunks and you'll be carried away by the cops,' I said. 'Do you have permission from Dirk to go swimming?' I went on sternly.

'The hell with Dirk,' the guy gobbled. 'He hired us, didn't he? It'll just be like a vacation, he said to us. And then what happens? Sam gets murdered. I might be the next one to get murdered.'

'So eat, drink and be merry, huh?' I turned and glared at the grinning Gale. 'You ought to be ashamed of yourself. Go play with Sandra for a while. She's looking lonesome over yonder.'

Gale trilled a dulcet laugh and shot away with the speed and agility of a fish. I gave Tripp a cigarette and sank down beside him.

'You'd like to see Sam's killer being caught, I guess?'

He looked at me and jutted out his thick underlip.

'I don't follow you, Muller. Sure, I want to see the killer caught. But what can I do that I'm not doing already?'

'I'm not certain, pal, you understand. I'm just fishing. I drop a line in here and a line in there. Then I go back round the lines, drawing them out, seeing if the bait has been taken and I'm left with nothing, or if I've caught some kind of fish. Do you follow me, Jude?'

'I don't think I do, Muller,' he replied slowly. 'Did you ever try shark-fishing?' he added with a sneer.

I could have tumbled him into the pool, swim-trunks or no swim-trunks. Somehow I controlled myself. I let a few minutes ride by. The sun seemed to be growing hotter. Gale had vacated the pool and was stretched out on an inflated couch beside Sandra. From where I was sitting the top half of the bikini had been dispensed with, so she could add another layer to that marvellous velvet tan.

Tripp had noticed this too and was straining his neck to get an eyeful. A thick vein throbbed in his throat.

'She's not wearing a damn thing!' he said in wonderment. 'This joint really drives a guy nuts.'

'Keep your cool, man,' I advised him. 'Listen,' I went on conversationally, 'remember the night Sandra was supposed to have seen someone in her room?'

'Do I what! There are some things you're meant never to forget, Muller. That's one of them, as far as I'm concerned.'

'Everybody had a ball? Where were you when it happened, Jude, baby?'

'Cut out that baby stuff, Muller,' he growled, squinting for a better look at Gale. 'Maybe I can bear you this close, but only just. I was in bed, naturally. I gotta sleep sometime, don't I.'

'You got up when you heard Sandra screaming?'

'You must be joking, mister! I got up? It's a wonder that'

scream wasn't heard at Long Beach. Course I got up. Everybody did.'

'Where was Sam when it happened?'

He left off drooling for a moment to give me a sharp stare.

'What are you driving at so late in the day? You're a private detective, ain't you? You're supposed to be tracking down the punk that started it all. Where do you hope to get if you do nothing but ask damnfool questions?'

'Sam was guarding Sandra's bedroom, wasn't he? Sitting at the door the way I found you sitting? Did he ever talk it over with you, Jude?'

Jude began to say something but then shrugged and went back to taking in the terrain. He feigned indifference.

'I'm not kidding, Jude,' I murmured. 'I want to know. If you don't open up when I'm smiling at you, I'll find some other way of loosening your tonsils.'

He stared at me again and his blunt features hardened belligerently. He raised a thick finger and pointed.

'Just because you caught Sam with a sucker punch, it doesn't mean you'll catch me, Muller.'

'I'm still smiling, jerk,' I said coldly. 'What did Sam say to you? He was right there by the door when Sandra screamed? But he was sleeping, wasn't he?'

Jude glanced away and shuffled his feet. 'It's hellish hot,' he said. 'I could do with a drink.'

'You'll drink when Dirk tells you to drink. You're only a puppet on a string, Jude honey. You do what you're told to do. You think when you're told to think. Why don't you search for that spark of individuality you were born with?'

Sweat was oozing to his broad forehead and he cuffed it off with a damp handkerchief.

'Sam was at the john,' he said in a strangled whisper.

'He told you so?'

'Yeah, he did. We were pals, weren't we? We were together for years and years. I'd never pull a dirty trick on a pal.'

'Forget it, chum. Your pal's dead. You want to see the killer locked up behind bars? I'm working to that end too, if you haven't noticed. The whole thing comes in a single package, Jude—Sandra's shadow and the murderer. So Sam took time off to go to the john, and he was there when he heard the scream?'

'I told you, didn't I?' he groaned. 'Now you'll go and tell Dirk. You'll tell Miss Marsh...'

'Don't you believe more than half of it, kiddo. But you should have told me this before. It says there really could have been a prowler in Sandra's bedroom. By the time it took Sam to get back he could have been and gone, right?'

Jude shook his head slowly and deliberately. 'Not according to Dirk, Muller. Dirk was on the spot as soon as Sam was. He didn't see anybody. We searched the whole house from top to bottom, and we didn't find anybody. Dirk said there had never been anyone in the bedroom but Miss Marsh herself. He—'

At that moment I heard feet shuffling behind us and turned to see the houseboy Hackett. He appeared highly agitated.

'Where is Miss Marsh?' he cried frantically. 'She's wanted on the telephone.'

I jumped up and grabbed the guy's arm. 'Who wants her, Hackett, and why all the steam?'

'It—it's that man again,' he panted. 'I'm sure it is, Mr Muller. I heard the voice once before, and—'

'All right,' I cut in on his waffle. 'Go tell her, Frank.'

It was all Sandra could do to walk round the perimeter of the swimming pool to join me. She reached out blindly and clutched my sleeve, hanging on like I was her last hope in the world.

'What am I going to do, Paul?' she groaned. 'I couldn't bear to listen to that maniac . . .'

She swayed and would have fallen if I hadn't steadied her with an arm about her waist. Gale had wrapped a length of terry towelling over her shoulders and bosom, and stood with her white teeth bared. There was something like pained shock reflected in her eyes.

'Pull yourself together,' I said to Sandra. 'Look how brave I am.'

'Nice advice if you can take it,' Gale commented. 'Did advice ever really solve anything? Darling, I wouldn't go near the phone,' she added to Sandra.

The TV star stared at her for several seconds, then she stared at me. A nerve fluttered briefly in her cheek.

'Gale is right, I suppose,' she shuddered. 'And I don't have to answer if I don't want to.'

'You don't have to do anything if you don't want to,' I said thinly. 'You could even bury your head in the sand. Come on and I'll go with you. The rest of you guys stay out of it.'

'Now wait a minute, Paul,' Gale began to object. 'I—'

'That means you as well,' I told her. 'Go flip your fins some more, honey.'

'I'm steadily becoming disillusioned with you,' the blonde said sweetly. 'I wonder why.'

I didn't answer her. I took Sandra on into the house and hoped we wouldn't meet Dirk Williams on the way. We didn't. I brought the dame to the lounge doorway.

'Where is that old fighting spirit, gorgeous?' I said with a grin. 'Remember that mule-kick you hung on me? Remember too that sticks and stones can break your bones, but names—'

'I can't do it, Paul,' she choked.

'You can. You're going to. Take the call in here. I'll go next door and listen to what's being said.'

She wavered in the doorway and I pushed her on into the room. She turned, hands gathered into fists and looked at me.

'Paul, this—this is going to be the last straw,' she whispered brokenly. 'I'm really going out of my mind.'

'Oh, sure,' I rasped in an ugly tone. 'Take the easy way out. Show the world what a weak-spined phoney you are when you haven't got a script to lean on. Answer the phone,' I added sharply. 'Hear what the latest bulletin is. I want to hear it as well, damn it. I'm entitled to some consideration.'

'Very well, Paul. But get ready for when I scream.'

'I am ready. I'm learning fast. I've got all the cotton-wool I need to stuff my ears.'

I went to the drawing-room, keeping my fingers crossed against the bad actor being here. It worked like a charm and he wasn't here. I sat down by the phone and picked up the receiver.

The voice of Sandra's tormentor was speaking to her—or rather it was the voice of one of her tormentors. It wasn't the guy I'd heard before and that I'd recognized as the may-hem merchant of White Surf Bay; this was the jerk with the oil-blob eyes speaking, the one I now knew to be Bill Gibson.

'... going to give you a break, Miss Marsh,' he was saying. 'You would welcome a break, wouldn't you? Well, speak up,' he rasped harshly when Sandra made no attempt to answer. Then, 'Look, lady, you're not trying to play it smart, I hope? You're not having this call traced back? If it's what you're doing, you're only wasting your time and making it tougher for yourself—'

'No, no, I'm not!' Sandra panted, just as I figured she must have gone dumb or fainted. 'Please—please leave me alone. What is it you want of me? You've threatened to kill me, but why—'

'Why, why, why!' the punk snarled at her. His voice was

edged with nervousness. 'Don't ask goddamn stupid questions. Get this straight. I'm willing to forget all I said to you, Miss Marsh. I'm willing to call the whole thing off. Does that register?'

'Yes, yes, it does. But how—'

'Hell, will you shut up and listen?' Gibson said grittily. 'How much would you be willing to pay to have the plan axed and be left alone from this out?'

I heard Sandra emit a long sigh. A sob caught in her throat. She said shakily, 'How—how much do you want?'

'That's keen, Miss Marsh. Real keen! Are you alone at this moment? Tell me nothing but the truth or else you'll suffer.'

'I am alone,' Sandra said evenly. 'How much money do you want from me?'

'I want fifty thousand dollars, lady. It's a lot of dough to the starving millions, but to you it's only peanuts. If you agree you'll never hear from me again. How does it sound?'

'I can hardly believe it,' Sandra gulped.

'Well, it can be an accomplished fact. But you must do exactly as I say, and you mustn't breathe a word of it to anyone. Do I get a gilt-edged promise?'

'Yes, yes! Just tell me when you want the money and where you want it delivered...'

Gibson laughed nastily. 'Take it easy. You get the dough wrapped up in a bundle, doll. Old bills, you understand. Nothing bigger than a hundred. And Miss Marsh—'

'Yes?' Sandra responded faintly.

'Don't even try taking a note of the serial numbers. I'll call you again soon. Then I'll tell you where I want the dough delivered. Do we have a deal?'

'Of course! But why—'

There was a sharp click and the line went dead. I jammed

the receiver down on its prongs and headed for the lounge. Sandra was sitting on a chair by the phone table, her green, hazel-flecked eyes staring off a thousand miles into space. I snapped my fingers under her nose.

'Okay, baby, he has gone away. You can come back down to earth again. Wakey, wakey.'

Her reaction was to shift her blank gaze fractionally until she was looking at me. Then she gave a whoop that sent icy tentacles curling round my spine. The whoop became a laugh —the laugh of the demented who has finally found freedom of a sort. The laughter rose in a thin, soaring spiral. I smashed my open hand against her cheek and the crazy sound stopped. She gaped at me in astonishment, then began blinking her eyes. Tears started welling in them and she bent her head to sob quietly.

'That's much better, Sandra,' I applauded.

I went to get her a drink. I was fitting the glass into her trembling fingers when Dirk Williams dashed into the room.

'What's going on here?' he hustled. 'Muller, what have you been doing to her this time?'

'What did I do to her last time?' I sneered.

'It's nothing to do with Paul,' the dame told him. 'There was another phone message, Dirk.'

'Remember what you promised, baby,' I said tautly.

Either she had forgotten or she just didn't care. While I stood there grinding my teeth in frustration she gave Williams the whole tale. I watched the guy's face as she talked. It hardened into a tight, bitter mask. For a second some other quality glittered in his eyes. Then he realized I was studying him and he dragged up his acting experience to take over. Which it did.

He slammed his right fist into the palm of his left hand.

'One more dirty trick,' he grated. 'Fifty thousand dollars!

Does he think we're nothing but a lot of nuts to swallow such a yarn? And what's this about remembering what she promised, Muller? You didn't hear what was said?'

'We've both heard what Sandra said, chum. The voice told her to play it cool, to keep it to herself.'

'So she hasn't kept it to herself? She's told me. Why shouldn't she tell me? Don't you think I'm to be trusted?'

I didn't answer that one. I left them both. Left the house and headed for the Jag. I was about to start the motor when Gale Bush ran round the corner of the house, waving at me to hold on.

'Paul, what happened? What was the phone call about? Where are you off to?'

'I wish I could go into the details,' I said. 'But I'm not in the mood. Sandra and Dirk can supply you with enough to keep you happy.'

'Is that your idea of a joke?' the dame griped. 'Look, wherever you're going, let me go with you. I don't give a damn if the roof is falling, and I sure could do with a break from all this intrigue. I'll ride in the trunk if you'd be embarrassed at having me ride side-saddle.'

'Some other time, baby. Right now I'm planning on a solo effort so I can think this whole thing out. If you've nothing better to do, you might go inside and hold Sandra's hand. You might even hold pal Dirk's while you're about it.'

She gave me a long look and caught her little pink tongue between her little white teeth.

'I'm getting a strong hunch about you, Paul,' she said accusingly. 'I've the feeling you're going to take off and never come back. You wouldn't pull a lousy trick, would you?'

'I promise to think about that too,' I told her and released the parking brake. She was muttering fiercely to herself as I went on towards the driveway leading to the road.

CHAPTER SIXTEEN

I drove into Burville and then, on reaching the town, I drove around in a fashion I wanted to be interpreted as aimless by anyone who had latched on to my tail. I didn't expect to prove attractive to a cop, but that was what happened—by courtesy of Sergeant Garson, no doubt. Garson trusted me the way he'd trust a snake in the grass. It was possible he figured I knew more about the Sam Walton caper than I'd told him; it was equally possible he was paying me a back-handed compliment, thinking I was away out ahead of the field as far as digging up clues was concerned, and intent on cashing in on my talent.

The cop wasn't wearing uniform, of course, nor was he at the wheel of an official car. It was a decrepit-looking heap he was driving, no doubt capable of doing a hundred, plus, at a pinch.

I dodged him all the same, and a little while later tooled the Jag past the Colonel and the Sunrise Studios. I was banking on a long shot, I knew, but it seemed the only source of the brand of information I needed that could be tapped without having the news whispered through the gloomy corridors of Hillview.

George Goldman was in and would see him in five minutes, I was told at the inquiry office. Goldman made it in exactly four minutes, sending out a message to come talk with him in his office

He shook hands and gave me a drink. He was puzzled about why I wanted to see him. He was a trifle anxious without being frightened, I thought. A little sheepish, too, on the side.

'I told Sandra you had called on me before, naturally,' he began. 'I knew you suspected me of all sorts of skulduggery. I just wanted to clear the air.'

'Forget it, George,' I said generously. 'This trip I'm asking you to do me a favour.'

'A favour—' He frowned and got a cigar going. Well, he couldn't commit himself, could he, until he learned what the favour was?

'Do you know which lawyer handles Sandra's affairs, George?'

'Yeah, I do,' he said cautiously. 'But why come all this distance to find out when you could have asked Sandra easily enough?'

'I didn't want to ask her. I've got a line on this case that I'm trying to follow up. Surely you want to do all you can to clear the air and have her back on the set in time to begin rehearsing for her new show? Do you realize the condition she's in at this minute, pal?' I added flatly.

George did. He sighed and chuffed at his cigar. He considered me earnestly for a half-minute, then he inclined his head.

'Yes, yes, I do, Paul. Sure I'll help you. I wish I could do more to help. Her lawyer is Jules Huntley. His office is on South Park Boulevard.'

'You know Huntley well?'

Goldman frowned some more. He nodded finally. 'Of course I know him well. He happens to be my own lawyer. I recommended Jules to Sandra when she talked about making a will.'

'She has made a will?'

'Hell, yes! But I don't understand you, Muller. What is this about? What are you driving at?'

'I'm just a little old private investigator, remember? Happens I might be able to break this ring of fear. If I do and the cops think kindly of me, we might be able to cover up no end of nasty gossip and rumour that would do your studios and your shining star absolutely no good.'

Goldman was eyeing me sceptically. It was plain he saw the advantages I was pointing out, all the same. He nodded again.

'Okay,' he said tautly, 'I'm listening.'

'Have you ever seen this will, George? You didn't witness it, maybe? Failing that, do you know who the beneficiaries would be in the event of something sad befalling Sandra?'

He seemed thunderstruck. He was hearing angles that had never occurred to him. He shook his head slowly, fighting off shock.

'This is getting crazier by the moment,' he said thickly. 'I understood you were following the line that grudge, spite, or jealousy was the motivation behind the phone calls, friend. Now you go off at a—a wild tangent...'

'I'm checking, buster,' I said bleakly. 'I may have a strong lead or I may not. The contents of that will can prove whether I'm right. Don't you *want* to help, for Pete's sake?'

He swallowed and looked guilty for a second, then he shrugged his big shoulders.

'All right, Paul,' he said meagerly, 'I'm with you. I don't know what's in the will. Only Sandra and Jules would know. And whoever witnessed the will,' he added feebly.

'And whoever the beneficiary is, maybe?' I nudged.

He jumped up from his chair and smashed his fist down on the helpless desk.

'Hells bells!' he frothed. 'This is taking things too far,

Muller. Are you suggesting I might benefit from Sandra's will if anything should happen to her—heaven forbid!'

'I didn't say so, George. Look, why don't you sit down calmly and smoke your cigar. Afterwards, when you stop behaving like a kid just out of kindergarten, why don't you give your old pal Jules a jingle and get him in the right mood for a visit from me?'

I thought he might swing all those busted knuckles at me, and for a couple of seconds he played with the idea. Then he subsided and gave a wan grin.

'Forgive me, Muller. But you took me on the raw just then.'

'You surely don't expect to be handled with talcum and diapers for all of your life, George? Give Jules a ring and butter him up for my visit.'

He reached for the phone and started dialling. Then he thought of something else and his index finger froze while he glanced up anxiously under his brows.

'There is one thing you must do for me in return, Paul. You must never, never breathe a word of this to Sandra.'

It was exactly what I wanted him to say. I crossed my heart and said I hoped a truck would run over me or a lightning bolt strike me if ever I did anything so lousy.

Satisfied, Goldman completed fingering the digits on the phone dial. There was a long delay before he was connected with the lawyer. At last he was and he went to work with a vengeance. I got a Lucky going while he talked. There was a nasty moment when the guy frowned and picked at his nose, worriedly.

'Oh, hell, Jules,' he snarled. 'I do you a favour and you do me a favour. And who sent you all that business, anyway? Tell me that!'

Evidently, Jules Huntley recalled who had sent all the business. Goldman grunted and chewed at his cigar. He said yes, and again, yes. Then he said, 'I can vouch for him myself. I'll take the rap if anything misfires at your end. You will? You will! Yeah, okay. Thanks, Jules. He's on his way.'

I was practically half-way there when he replaced the receiver and saw me grabbing the door handle.

'Just remember, Paul, You're dealing with dynamite. If you're not discreet as blazes Jules and I will catch it in the neck. If there is a repercussion, it'll hit you too no matter which hole you crawl into.'

'You know something, George,' I said warmly, 'you're a real sweet baby. If the gag develops the way I hope it will develop, you're going to have a dewy-eyed damsel on your doorstep one of these mornings, just raring to go.'

Goldman was chewing his cigar dubiously as I passed out and closed the door behind me.

A little later saw me cruising into South Park Boulevard. It was a street occupied mostly by lawyers, real estate agents, marketing agents, and no doubt a few shysters. I found a slot to leave the Jag, and twenty minutes afer departing from Goldman I was ensconced with a fat party who said his name was Jules Huntley, and who offered me a cold and clammy hand before offering me a chair in front of his desk. Anyhow, the lawyer had been suitably primed, and when he had checked my licence to make sure I really was the Paul Muller Goldman had spoken of, we got down to the subject of Sandra Marsh's will.

Suffice to say it was an eye-opener, and proved I was still good for the occasional reliable hunch. A little later I was holding Huntley's clammy paw some more and assuring him that my reputation was such that the last thing I could indulge in was careless talk and the breaking of confidences.

Back on the street I lit a cigarette and considered the layout of the territory. It seemed much the same as when I'd arrived, and showed that Garson's bloodhounds didn't get nearly enough practice to be effective.

I went to the Jag and drove to a bar. I ordered a Scotch on the rocks to help me mull things over. According to Larry Stern, the brothers Gibson had their headquarters currently in Anfield. Did it mean that one or both of them commuted between Anfield and Burville for the purpose of their present plan? I didn't know and there was no reliable way of finding out. It meant then that I must play my music by ear.

I didn't risk going back to Hillview, where the cops would certainly glue on again and maybe cramp my style later. Instead, towards dusk I shut myself in a phone booth and raised the macabre mansion. It was Hackett who answered my call and I asked him to go fetch Sandra.

'Don't make a song and dance about it, Frank, and pass the same hint to Miss Marsh.'

'I understand perfectly,' the guy said. 'You might like to know that the police have been here again, Mr Muller.'

'Oh. What did they want?'

'They asked more questions. They wondered where you are.'

'I bet they did, Frank. But they've gone?'

'Yes, sir, they have. But Miss Bush says she noticed two plainclothes men patrolling the grounds.'

'No kidding?' I grunted. 'How do you know they're cops, Frank? Did they report to the house?'

They hadn't reported to the house, Hackett said. But Miss Bush had approached one of the men and ordered him to show her his identification. He had done so and there was no doubt the men were police officers.

'All right, Frank. Fetch Miss Marsh.'

'Paul!' she cried a minute later. 'Where are you? I've been close to distraction. The police have been here. They left two guards behind. Well, they must be guards, and—'

'I know all that, baby,' I interrupted her. 'Hackett was good enough to put me in the picture. So what's wrong with cops? They ought to be what your morale needs about now.'

'Oh, it's not that I don't appreciate their presence. I do, of course. But it tends to underline the whole sordid affair. Next thing I know we'll have newspaper reporters! When are you coming back here, Paul?'

'Not for a little while,' I told her.

'Why?' she wailed. 'I don't feel safe when you're not around. It's funny how you seem to exude strength and confidence.'

'That's me right enough,' I said modestly. 'Big and strong and exuding confidence. But what's so funny about it? No, don't bother to tell me. Like I said, peach blossom, I won't be home for a spell. I'm busy.'

'Then you—you've found a clue? Well, it is what a detective looks for, isn't it?'

'Yeah,' I said. 'It's what I'm looking for. And, Sandra, don't mention I was ringing if you don't have to. Those cops haven't got the blind faith in me that you have. By the way, you haven't heard any more from the guy who wants to sell you fifty thousand bucks' worth of relief?'

She hadn't, she said. That was another point we had to discuss. What would she do if he did ring with instructions on where and when to deliver the money?

'Just take the message and tell him you're ready to act according to his orders.'

'All right, Paul,' she rejoined weakly. 'But Dirk says he would rather die himself than part with a single penny to the crook.'

'Oh yeah? But it isn't Dirk's life that's been threatened. Where is he at the moment?'

'He's out,' she answered. 'He said he needed a short drive to help him sort matters into a sensible pattern. I didn't have the heart to ask him to stay. He's bearing this all so stoically, Paul.'

'He's a great guy. Where's Jude?'

'Not too far away. He's wonderful too. He never leaves me. He's just like a—a—'

She didn't finish, but I knew what she meant. Like a great pet dog. I said that was fine and to keep her chin up. Then I said goodbye and hung up. I went out to the Jag and set off through the mellow dusk for the Anfield highway.

It was around ten when I drove into the town and cruised through a lot of back streets to reach West Nation. I parked a dozen yards from the front of 684, got out, lit a cigarette and paused for a few minutes to allow the dust to settle.

When the scenery had been thoroughly assimilated I moved on to the hallway of the apartment building. A dump was the most generous verdict I could give it. A dimly-lit, fusty-smelling fleapit that had somehow been bypassed by the march of progress.

There was a row of mailboxes on each side of the hallway and I scanned them, starting on the left. I saw the name, 'W. Gibson', the 'W' probably standing for William. W. Gibson or Bill Gibson was housed in 5c, and if I wanted to get there, there was only one way it could be done—by climbing the stairs that left the well of the hall and vanished in the overhead murk.

I started climbing.

On the fifth floor I trod a passage that was covered by a ghastly yellow strip of linoleum. However, it would take me to the Gibson boys' apartment, so why complain?

I pressed the buzzer with my left thumb and got a firm grip on the .38 in my pocket. No joy. I pressed again and kept up the presssure for a while. I heard the buzzer going inside the apartment, but nothing else. I tried the door and bingo, it opened when I turned the handle and pushed.

Darkness. An atmosphere. I pushed the door until it swung back its full distance, then took a tentative step inside. Here was a short hall, with the doors leading off it. I opened the one in front of me and saw a toilet basin, a towel lying on the floor. There was no one in the bathroom. Next I opened the door on my right. Here was a small living-room reeking of stale cigarette smoke.

I fumbled for the light switch and snapped it on, then, on the next instant, almost wished I hadn't. Bill Gibson was at home right enough. He was reclining on a battle-weary sofa, one hand trailing on the floor, one foot doing likewise. The oil-blob eyes were open, staring fixedly at the ceiling. The trouble was they weren't seeing anything. A wicked-looking dagger protruding from the guy's stomach told you why.

In a situation such as this my first instinct is to run like hell and not stop to query the whys and wherefores. But I was on a trail and I had to keep going to the bitter end.

All the same, when I did begin to search I didn't loaf around. I started in the living-room and worked my way through to the bedrooms. There were two of them—neither of them big enough to whip a cat in—and I struck gold-dust in the second one. It was a tiny, sophisticated transmitter and it was tucked away on the top shelf in the closet.

I put it into my pocket, then wiped off everything I'd touched. Back in the living-room I had a last look at Bill. It was enough to make even the toughest private eye throw up. I left while my stomach was making up its mind, closed the outer door gently, and commenced the long journey to the ground floor.

Luck was with me and all was still quiet. There was a wall phone at the end of the hall and I dialled police headquarters.

A tired voice answered me and wanted to know who was speaking.

'Get this straight first time round, I said quickly. 'Right? Come to six-eight-four, West Nation Street and pick up a corpse.'

There was some kind of choking sound at the other end of the line. A thick cough.

'Hey, what is this? Who are you? What—'

I hung up at that juncture, had a brief gander around me, then set off for the street.

I had gained the doorway when a dame came towards the apartment house, head down, striding purposefully. She walked into me full tilt, then drew back and wheeled to take it on the lam. I grabbed her arm, held her until she gave up struggling. Then I said, 'Well. if it isn't my old bed-mate, Alice! Fancy meeting you here. It sure is a small world, isn't it?'

'No, no!' she gasped in a horrified tone. 'Please, Paul, you can't rope me into anything...'

'Like to make a small bet? Let's drift to my car.'

She struggled for another few seconds, then shrugged and gave in. I took her to the Jag, pushed her on to the front passenger seat and dropped in beside her. She sat straight and tense while I gunned the motor and got out of that street fast.

'Where are you taking me, Paul?'

'Let me see. We could go and watch a ball game at the stadium, if there was a ball game playing at the stadium. On the other hand we might nip out to White Surf Bay and put up at one of those cute beach-huts. But what am I saying! White Surf Bay. Beach hut. There's a weirdo connotation there someplace. Now I've got it. We were playing something called Bumps on the Head and Screams from the Bedroom. I was getting all the bumps and you were giving with the screams. I wonder why, baby. I really do wonder why. After all, if I was having those goddamn bumps, then I should have been the one screaming. It's logic, isn't it?'

'Stop it, you sadistic sonofabitch!'

I drove until we reached the opposite side of town, then I nosed the car into an alley, cut the engine and the lights. The alley was a dim, narrow canyon where few people ventured after dusk. Alice made a dive for the door handle on her side and catapulted in frustration when the door wouldn't open.

'Special locking device, honey. I had it installed for the first phoney I wanted to beat to death in the heap. You get a kick out of killing someone in a car. Ever tried it? But of course you haven't. You go for the fun of the chase, the hunting and the harrying before you administer the *coup de grace.*'

Alice commenced sobbing.

'What the hell *are* you talking about, Paul?' she panted. 'All right! I went along with Bill and Walt. They talked me into picking you up, sailing in your boat, shacking up with you in that beach-hut—'

'You've just done something terrible to my pride, Alice, but we'll let it drift. I'll simply ask you why.'

'I don't know why. They said it was part of a deal. There was money in it for all three of us. They promised me no one would get hurt. I didn't want you to get hurt, Paul. I really didn't!'

She sobbed some more and I passed her over a handkerchief. A little later I urged her to talk and not stop until she had filled me in thoroughly. She stuck to her story. There had been a plan, naturally. They had been watching me for days, maybe weeks, studying my habits, the places I visited. Then the scene was set at the Bluebell. She had done what her brothers schooled her to do. I might have been hurt a little, but I hadn't been hurt that badly, had I?

'And you don't know what it was in aid of, sugar?' I said grimly. 'Yet you're bound to have heard Walt threaten what might happen to me if I didn't duck out of a case I hadn't even taken? That was their first big mistake, honey-chile, and it shows what rank amateurs they are. Or should I say were?'

She gripped my arm and her fingers dug in fiercely.

'Were! What are you saying, Paul? Do you mean they've been snatched by the cops?'

'One thing at a time, Alice. And please remove your talons before I break your arm at the elbow. Now,' I grated when she had retreated to the extremity of the seat, 'do you solemnly swear you were ignorant of what your kin were up to?'

'I'll swear it anywhere you please,' she said vehemently. 'I was in the bedroom with Bill and I didn't hear what Walt was saying to you. Sure, I knew they wanted to put some sort of pressure on you. Bill wouldn't explain, but he did say it was nothing but a gag to confuse you...'

I'd the feeling she was telling me the truth. After all, what had the brothers to gain apart from causing me confusion? They hadn't set out to kill me or maim me. They had made a show of scaring me off Sandra Marsh. Did they think I would stay scared? It didn't seem likely. They had been told to do something and they'd done it. They had been nothing but clumsy tools in the hands of someone who figured he was a psychologist.

Confuse me. Frighten me. Have me wondering about the identity of the person holding the manipulating strings. Did he have an in with Sandra or didn't he? If he didn't have an in with the dame, then how did he know so much; how could he take steps to frustrate a move that hadn't begun to happen?

The more I thought of it the more probable it seemed that the puppet master hoped I would add it all up later in the

game, and come to the conclusion he wanted me to come to
—that George Goldman was Sandra's tormenting shadow.

The phone call when I'd been talking with Sandra in her
bedroom at the Hotel Rialto had been just another psychologi-
cal touch to send me astray. It was crazy, of course. Crazy and
juvenile. It pointed to a mixed-up psyche if ever I'd heard of
one. Laughable if it wasn't so tragic. Well, you can't laugh
off a couple of killings unless you've got a pretty gruesome
sense of humour.

Alice's pleading voice crawled into my thoughts.

'What are you going to do with me, Paul? You'll give me
a break, won't you? I should never have listened to my
brothers. They were always dabbling in something they knew
little about.'

'Who were they working for, doll?'

'Who— Why ask me? I don't know. Honest, I don't, Paul.
They didn't tell me anything.'

'Where is Walt about now, baby?'

She shook her head violently. She didn't answer me.

'Okay,' I grunted and reached for the ignition switch. 'If
you won't talk to me you'll talk to the cops.'

She clawed at my hand and began sobbing again.

'Why can't you believe anything I tell you?' she shrilled.
'I don't know. You called at their apartment, didn't you. Were
they not there? But that's a stupid question, isn't it. I—'

'Did you live with your brothers, Alice?' I broke in curtly.

'No, of course I didn't. I've got an apartment of my own out
in the north side. I've got a job too, working at a club.'

'Not the Bluebell?'

She shuddered and took the cigarette I offered her.'

'Not the Bluebell. The Golden Flame. I've got a singing
spot. It's what I've wanted to do all of my life. Sing. Can you
beat it, Paul?' She giggled hysterically. 'Just sing!'

'Keep doing it,' I urged. 'When did you visit your brothers last?'

'Two days ago,' she said without hesitation.

'You didn't visit their apartment tonight?'

'I told you, didn't I?'

'Why were you going there tonight?'

'Oh, hell, you talk like a cop, Paul. But what do I expect,' she went on musingly. 'You are a cop of sorts. Still, you were an awful nice experience.'

'I wish I could say the same for you, honey,' I said regretfully. 'Now listen to this, Alice, and listen good. I've got a lead on this runaround. Whether or not you know it, your brothers were helping a certain character to frighten Sandra Marsh right out of her brains—'

'Sandra Marsh!' Alice panted. 'The TV star? Paul, I can't believe it—'

'Suit yourself. You're getting the facts. Here are some more. Last night one of your brothers—Bill, I'm sure—killed a man at Sandra Marsh's home outside Burville. And tonight, Alice, somebody has been to that apartment you saw me leaving and stuck a dagger into Bill's belly.'

She gasped and I figured she had fainted. She hadn't, though. She said hoarsely, 'Is—is he dead?'

'As dead as can be, doll. So the plot thickens. So the gag begins to turn sour. You're sure you didn't go there earlier, have a row with Bill, and pull the knife on him?'

'No, no, no!'

'I asked you before and I'm asking you again, Alice. Why were you visiting the apartment tonight?'

It seemed that an age ran by before she answered in a dull, lifeless tone. 'I was promised money. Five hundred dollars. They never paid me... Oh, Paul, this is terrible! Bill dead.

Murdered. Who killed him—Walt? The party they were working for?'

'I don't know,' I told her. I started up the engine and drove
out of the alley. At which Alice threatened to blow her top.

'Where are you taking me, Paul? Not to the police! But I
don't know anything. I didn't do anything...'

I said nothing until we were in midtown Anfield. Then I
drew in at the curb and released the lock on the dame's side.
She looked at the door and then she looked at me.

'You're letting me go?' she whispered throatily.

'I don't have any room in my gallery for your type, honey.
It's a drag, isn't it. One last word. I put an anonymous call
through to the cops, reporting your brother's murder. I'd
advise against going back there to check my story. I'd advise
you to make the best of a bad deal. Understand?'

She leaned over impulsively and kissed my cheek. It was
like being kissed by a lump of ice. Then Alice snatched the car
door open and was gone.

I got back to Hillview around midnight. I had just killed
the Jag's engine and climbed out when a couple of shadows
closed in on me from two sides. I recognized Garson and some
other dick who was a stranger.

'You mean you never go to sleep when you're working on
a case, chief?' I said witheringly.

'Cut out that witty crap, mister,' Garson growled. He gripped
my arm and led me away from the front of the house until
we were surrounded by shadows. 'Now, Muller,' the Sergeant
went on, 'where have you been since you left here about dusk?'

'You must be joking! I'm not a free agent? I don't have the
rights enjoyed by the ordinary citizen?'

'Not when you're mixed up in murder, you don't,' the cop
snarled. 'I had a man on your tail. You spotted him. You

ducked out on him. Why, if you've got a clear conscience?'

'Why don't you just be your age?' I grated. 'I go where I damn-well like. I'm a private investigator with a client. I've got obligations to that client. If you want to know where I was and what I was doing, I'll tell you. I was in town—Burville town, that is. I did a round of some bars to relieve the tedium. After which I lost my way and finished up in a cathouse. Well, didn't you ever get lost, Sarge, and finish up in a cathouse?'

Garson winced. He clicked his teeth together savagely.

'You weren't near your own back yard tonight, buster—Anfield?'

'Of course I wasn't. But what if I was? I can't drop in on my home town if I feel like it?'

'A guy was killed over there tonight,' Garson explained tersely. 'Stabbed with a dagger.'

'You don't say. So when somebody gets killed in Anfield, you naturally gravitate to Paul Muller? Do me a favour, will you, chief—go suck a lemon.'

I left them on that note, hearing Garson clicking his teeth to beat a band. The front door was closed but it opened as soon as I gave the bellpush a jab. Hackett let me in.

'Good night, Mr Muller.'

'Hi, Frank.' The hall was empty. I jerked my head for Hackett to follow me into the drawing-room. He followed me obediently and I closed the door gently behind us.

'What is it, Mr Muller?' he asked anxiously.

'I don't know, Frank. I really don't. Where are the dames—I mean Miss Marsh and Miss Bush?'

'They've both gone to bed. Miss Marsh asked me to give you a message. There haven't been any further telephone calls.'

'Is that the message, pal, or is it an original contribution?'

'The message,' he said thinly and coloured slightly.

I patted his shoulder and gave him a Lucky. I asked him

where Jude was at. I might have known without asking. He was stationed outside Miss Marsh's bedroom.

'How about Dirk. Did he get back yet?'

'No,' Frank told me. 'He hasn't come back. Would you like me to inform Miss Marsh you have returned?'

'Don't bother. I'm beaten myself. I'm going up to bed.'

I gave Frank another Lucky and left him. He was standing in the hall when I glanced back down the stairs at him. He was scratching his head thoughtfully. Likely he was trying to figure out how many kooks could stir a broth without all of them being locked up.

I found Jude in position on his chair at Sandra's door. He was snoring gently and I didn't have the heart to kick one of the chair legs. Instead I catfooted on to the door of Dirk Williams' bedroom, twisted the handle and stepped inside. With the door shut I flipped the light switch and began a systematic search.

It took me fifteen minutes to find what I was looking for. Dirk had hidden the small radio receiver under the bed mattress. It showed how little ingenuity the guy really had, but then he was so damn smug and sure of himself he didn't reckon anyone suspected him.

I froze when somebody tapped on the bedroom door. I had the .38 clear and ready to use when the door opened slowly and Gale Bush stared in at me.

'Paul Muller!' she cried sibilantly. 'What are you doing here? Why are you pointing that gun at me?' she went on fearfully.

'Purely reflex action,' I assured her with a grin and stuck the weapon under my waistband. 'What am I doing here? Yeah ... Well, I wanted to have a word with Mr Handsome, and as I couldn't find him downstairs I figured he might have gone to bed. Satisfied, cute lips, or do I have to dream up a better excuse?'

I had laid the receiver on the dressing-table where all Dirk's brushes and deodorants and stuff were scattered, and the dame's gaze shuttled to it.

'What is that?'

She was crossing swiftly to the dressing-table when I grabbed up the instrument and pushed it into my pocket.

'Just my shaver, honey. Sometimes I carry it around with me.'

'Paul,' she said with a catch in her voice, 'you are acting very strangely. What is it? What is the matter? You know you can trust me, don't you?'

'Sure I can, Gale. And right now I'm trusting you to go back to bed and mind your own business. Not a word to Dirk, remember.'

She nodded. Her cheeks had gone very pale and her lips had gone dry enough to warrant their being licked by a small pink tongue. She backed off to the door, her eyes wide and filling with a dawning comprehension, as the stylish writers like to say.

In the doorway she paused, wanting to say something else to me. She didn't make it. She drew the door shut and was gone.

I acted swiftly now, replacing things I had shifted, bundling some jackets into the closet, kicking back the shoe-trees. I was studying the effect, preparatory to taking off myself when the room door opened again.

'Muller!' Dirk Williams snarled at me while a nerve snapped viciously in his cheek. 'What the hell are you doing in my bed-room? This is the final straw,' he ranted wildly. 'This I will not stand under any circumstances whatever.'

'None?' I said curiously and brought the radio receiver

from my pocket. I extended it in the palm of my hand.
Williams turned ashen.

'Where—where—' he gobbled.

'Under your mattress, punk. And take a look here,' I went
on casually, producing the transmitter I'd taken from Bill
Gibson's apartment in Anfield. 'What do you suppose this is—
something to blow out your brains with? You should hope,
pal!'

He rushed at me and slung a crisp uppercut to the angle of
my jaw. It connected too and slewed me into a tight, driving
circle. Heady with success, he aimed a kick at my groin. That
one didn't connect, because I hate being hit where it really
hurts. The next rush he made I frustrated with a hammer-
blow under the heart. He choked and took on a couple of
shades of green. I pulled the follow-up slightly. When I'm
really mean I can put a guy to sleep for an hour, and I didn't
want Dirk to sleep that long. The breath whooshed from his
lungs and he tumbled to the beige carpet.

The door opened once more and Gale Bush peered in.

She said, 'Moses!' in a stricken voice and went away.

I gave Dirk a dig in the ribs with my toe.

'Get up, punk.'

'I can't, I can't! You've ruined me...'

'Ruined is right, buster,' I gritted at him.

I took a handful of his shirtfront and hauled him to his
feet. He swayed, aimed a feeble punch at me and fell back
on to a chair. I drew up another chair before him.

'Listen, slug. The game is up. I've got all the angles off pat,
so you needn't waste your breath arguing.'

'You're wrong,' he whimpered. 'Wrong! I found that receiver. I found it in Sandra's bedroom. I took it away in case
she saw it and threw a fit...'

'Yeah, you did, didn't you? You took it away when it had

served its purpose. Only it was you who put it there in the first place, Dirk baby. Billy Gibson was on the other end of it out in the grounds, doing your bidding, scaring the hell out of Sandra, trying to send her crazy!'

'No, no!'

'I told you not to argue, louse. It all started off as a gag to have Sandra certified. She has settled two million bucks on your sweetie-pie Gale. Gale gets the dough if Sandra dies or is otherwise totally incapacitated. She would have been incapacitated fine shut up in a bughouse. It was a screwy clause for anybody to put in a will, but then, like I keep telling everybody, you never know with dames...'

'You're a liar, Muller. A dirty liar—'

'We'll see, Dirk. Let me continue. At the outset the idea might have been to kill Sandra, but you baulked, or maybe Gale did. It could be she doesn't go for murder. But this is murder, chum.

'You hired the Gibson lads to create confusion and to make appropriate noises over the phone and the radio. You went into Sandra's bedroom in the middle of the night, when you knew Sam Walton was at the john. You made sure Sandra saw your shape in the darkness before you pulled out. That was a neat trick and calculated to plant the seeds of insanity in her mind.

'You pretended to love Sandra, but you never loved her punk. Likely she was too much woman for you. Gale was more your size and more suited to your limitations—'

'You bastard, Muller. You dirty lying bastard...'

He was frothing at the mouth now, his dark eyes darting this way and that like those of a cornered rat.

'As I told you, Dirk, we'll see. You had Bill Gibson lurking in the grounds. You had Sam Walton posted there too. You hired those chumps to build a front for yourself. But you didn't reckon on Sam spotting Gibson. Bill blew his cool when he figured there was the risk of being caught. He had a gun with him, which was a mistake, and he used it to shoot Sam. You should be proud of yourself, I guess. You plotted the yarn and wrote the script. You hired the cast—one set to act as the goodies and the other as the baddies. But you never meant they should come to grips in earnest. Yet they did, and like I said, Bill Gibson shot Sam Walton.'

'Lies! All lies! You can't prove a cursed word of it.'

'I'm not finished, jerk. Gibson made his getaway and headed back to Anfield. Then he developed a case of cold feet. Well, a murder rap can be somewhat embarrassing. But Bill was nothing if not dogged. He dreamed up a gag of his own. He would touch Sandra for fifty grand and promise an end to the harassment before taking off. He did so. You heard all about it from Sandra, and naturally, Dirk, you just had to break a spoke in Bill's wheel. You drove to Anfield, bringing a dagger along for the ride, which you left pinned to Bill's belly button. I was there tonight, pal. I found the transmitter you gave Bill to use. This is it here. Also,' I lied blithely, 'Bill wasn't quite dead when I arrived. He was able to name you as his assailant before he cashed his chips.'

It was the instant Dirk picked to utter a mad yell and dash for the door. I tried to stop him, but I wasn't nearly quick enough. He gained the corridor as I lunged after him.

CHAPTER SEVENTEEN

I tilted—head first, almost—into the massive figure of Jude Tripp. Jude had been brought awake by the fuss and lumbered along to find out what was cooking. He allowed Williams to pass him, naturally, and immediately gathered I was planning on having the bad actor's scalp.

'Take it easy there, Muller,' he growled ferociously.

'Hold him, Jude,' Dirk panted back over his shoulder. 'He's gone crazy or something.' And so saying, he bounded on to reach the top of the stairs.

'Out of my way, ugly,' I snarled at Jude. 'That guy is a killer and we've got to catch him before he does more damage.'

'Oh yeah!' the mutt sneered. 'You know, Muller, I always did figure you had a coupla bolts missing.'

He made a grab at me and I ducked the other way. As he turned with all the supple grace of a Saracen tank I belted him hard in the bread basket. He didn't like it. He gave a couple of inches of ground. It wasn't enough to get past him and join Dirk, so I rapped him sharply on the left ankle, and as he bounced about on one leg I cuffed him on the jaw. That made a gap for me to get through.

I ran fast. Even so, Dirk was half-way down the staircase when I reached the top of it. A lot of things happened then in short order. I glimpsed Frank Hackett crossing the hall to open the front door. He opened the door and Sergeant Garson and his pal came in. There was another guy at the back of the pair, and his intention seemed to be to get past the cops, come hell or high water.

'This chump says he wants to see Dirk Williams,' Garson announced to Hackett. 'He won't give his name, and—'

'My name is Walt Gibson,' the gatecrasher said harshly. 'I want to see Williams. I've got something here that Williams needs badly.'

By then Dirk had dashed on down to the hall, but the intruder appeared to change his mind about having anything to do with the hall. The bad actor wheeled and began climbing the stairs again. He saw me and gave a keening wail of frustration.

'Help me, Muller. Help me!'

'There you are, Williams,' Walt Gibson shouted. 'You had to gum everything up, hadn't you? You went to Anfield tonight and stuck a knife in Bill...'

'No, no! I didn't.'

Dirk clattered back down the stairs, spun at the bottom to make a break for the rear of the house. Nobody reckoned on how Walt Gibson would react. With a howl of fury he pulled a gun and began shooting.

Garson and his pal scattered instinctively at the first shot. The first shot struck the stair rail and sent slivers of wood whining every which way. The second shot was taken with more care and Dirk Williams emitted a high-pitched shriek of agony.

Garson recovered and flung himself on the gunman. His pal rushed to his aid and between them they bore Gibson to the floor. In a few seconds Garson had possession of the gun. He turned a tight face in my direction.

'What kind of madhouse is this? Go see if the guy is hurt.'

'You've just got to be fooling, Sarge.'

I went on down to Dirk all the same. He was writhing

about on the floor, both hands pressed to his chest.

'He got me, Muller. He got me. I'm going to die—'

'You've a hell of a lot to say for a dying man, Dirk.'

Hackett materialized to assist, as did Jude Tripp. The fat man was making queer sounds and his eyes reflected total disillusion.

'I got caught up in a bum deal, didn't I?' he mourned.

'Maybe you'll listen to your betters next time, slob,' I told him.

A weak cry drifted down the staircase.

'What is going on?' Sandra Marsh demanded in a dazed voice. 'Who was shooting? What has happened? Gale! Where are you going to—'

As she cried this I glanced at the open doorway where Gale Bush, clad in slacks and sweater, was hurrying out to the night. On being spotted by Sandra, the petite blonde broke into a fast run. I left Dirk to the care of Hackett and Tripp and took after her.

'Hey, you come back here,' Garson raved. 'Muller!' he screamed. 'I command you to halt.'

Out of the house, I couldn't see a thing for a moment. Then I was able to make out plenty—shadows, starshine. A cool breeze soughed down from the hills.

I heard the dim patter of running feet. They were making for the corner of the house where the garages were located. I had gained the corner when I heard a car door slamming. A motor crashed to life, revved, roared. Twin headlamps spat at me from the gloom, and the next thing the sports car was raging straight at me.

I flung myself sideways—just in the nick of time, to coin a phrase—and the sports car zoomed past me, Gale Bush laughing mockingly like she had bust all of her gaskets.

She surged towards the driveway leading to the road, took

the bend on two wheels. I winced at the screeching of pun-
ished tyres. The car righted itself and tore on. I ran to the Jag
and leaped in behind the joystick. My own headlamps reflected momentarily on the rear of the sports car before it
took another bend.

The dame was crazy for driving that way. Unless she slowed
she would never reach the entrance gate. But so what? Everybody was crazy at this damn dump.

I had gone only a hundred yards when I heard it. There was
a sound of fierce braking, then a sickening crumpling noise.
I tramped on the accelerator, swept round a bend, and threw
out the anchors.

Just as I'd figured. The sports car had slithered off the
driveway and finished up entangled with a tree trunk. A
thin sob emerged from the wreckage. There was a thick stench
of petrol and the whole works could burst into flames at any
second.

I scrambled from the Jag and went to extricate Gale. I lifted
her and carried her a safe distance before lowering her gently
to the ground. Her arms tried to cling to my neck, but they
didn't have much strength and soon fell away.

'Take it easy,' I told her.

'I—I was a fool, Paul, wasn't I?'

'Yeah, you were. Look, you're going to need a medico.
Garson might have put a call through for help, but again, he
might not. Lie still here until I get back.'

'No!' she panted. 'Don't leave me alone, Paul.' Her voice
faded to a gurgling whisper. 'You're—a—good guy, Paul ...'

'I'm a wow,' I said feebly. 'Don't talk. Save your breath.'

'For what?' she said bitterly. 'I should have been satisfied
and waited. She never did me any harm. Just smothered me,
kind of. She should have had a sister... Then Dirk talked
me into it. I listened to him... Hell, Paul, it's getting dark

... cold .. Hold my hand ...'

I held her hand. There wasn't much life in it. I heard sirens in the distance. So Garson had put a call in for the police and an ambulance. Would the ambulance get here in time?

'Hold my hand, Paul.'

'It's what I'm doing, doll.'

'I can't feel it. I can't feel a thing.'

The sirens were coming closer. They reached the entrance to the driveway and stormed through. I heard someone running from the house, looked up and made out the form of Sandra Marsh.

'Paul, Paul! Did she crash? Is she hurt?'

'Get out of here,' I snapped. 'Do you want to be knocked down by those vehicles.

They howled along the driveway, a squad car out front, an ambulance tailing it. The squad car braked hard and the ambulance ran on into the back of it. They separated with a tearing of metal.

Sandra brushed past me to kneel beside Gale. She moaned and leaned over to peer into the blonde's face.

'Gale, Gale! Can you hear me, sweetheart? Speak to me. Oh, no! No, she's not—'

She was. She lay there, small and fragile, totally inanimate. A white-coated intern gripped my sleeve.

'Let's see what we can do—'

'There's nothing you can do here, buster. Better go on to the house and you'll find somebody there to baby up.'

'Let's go, Sandra,' I said brusquely.

She didn't answer me. She didn't even know I was there. She had Gale's body cradled in her arms and she was rocking it the way a mother would rock a child, crooning all the while.

At that instant the sports car burst out in lurid flame.